Deadly Gold

By the same author

Lawless Hideout
Desert Trails
Hell-Bent Gents
Colt Flame
Kiowa Blood
The Killer Stamp
Killer's Greed
Frontier Murder
Revenge in Montana
Joe Killer
Sheriff Sixsmith
Tequila Man
Young Gunnies
Shard at Lynchburg

Deadly Gold

JOHN BLAZE

A Black Horse Western

ROBERT HALE · LONDON

© John Blaze 2000
First published in Great Britain 2000

ISBN 0 7090 6717 8

Robert Hale Limited
Clerkenwell House
Clerkenwell Green
London EC1R 0HT

Typeset by
Derek Doyle & Associates, Liverpool.
Printed and bound in Great Britain by
WBC Book Manufacturers Limited, Bridgend.

ONE

He was riding alone, an exercise he had not taken for some weeks; his big-boned mount plodded slowly, something that suited Kurt Kallon because he wanted to think. He wanted to think about his choice of partners in what would be a mad grim trail after three stinking killers. Actually there hadn't been much choice. His partners had been wished on him! He figured old man Fate had pushed him into this three-some!

As a big lanky range-hand, ex-sheriff, ex-wrestler, he didn't usually waste much time on reflection but there were times when a man had to think – and this was one of them. For the first time in weeks his two partners were not riding like shadows on both sides of him. Not that his two unusual partners really bothered him!

He was miles from Cragside. He'd have to get there before sundown, he figured, before his two partners went out on some fool mission of their own to get a lead on the killers of their brother.

'Hey, Big Feller – time we got a move on!' Kurt always called his horse Big Feller and the damned brute always knew when he was trying to communicate. Ears pricked up and the animal went into a lope.

The rough ground under the hooves resounded to the thud-thud. Not that the distant hills around Cragside seemed much closer.

Kurt gave a muttered curse. He had wasted too much time on the bum lead he had been given. He had been told that three ragged ornery cusses had made trouble near the Fort Worth area – in the community always called Cowtown – near the Stockyards Hotel – a joint where the bar stools were really saddles perched on round wood supports, but the hellions had turned out to be useless rogues who had been drunk for a week. They didn't match the descriptions of the three ugly bastards who had killed Billy.

So it was time wasted. And his rear was saddle-sore. His belly seemed empty of grub. He could relish a big steak, rare and red, with onions and new spuds and gravy. And maybe a big jug of ale. Maybe he should get drunk. But his two partners didn't approve of that. Well, they wouldn't!

The damned sun was sinking too fast for riding comfort in a land where cholla cactus grew waist-high and clawed at man and beast if they rode too close. The blue shadows of the rocks of Cragside still seemed a long way distant but he knew he had knocked off a few miles with the fast lope; now the horse was beginning to steam.

He came out of the rock- and sand-filled gully and at once nearly rode down the old galoot with the dying burro. Kurt Kallon knew the animal was almost dead. The oldster was trying to pull the critter along by the reins. Even as Kurt hauled in and stared, the burro gave an agonized howl, fell, and lay on its side with its belly heaving and saliva on the mouth. The oldster cursed and raised his stick.

'Giddup, durn yuh!'

Kurt strode over and yanked the wood from the man's dirty hand.

'That brute is as good as dead! What the hell have you been doing with it?'

'I was in a hurry. Got to git to the assayer's office in Cragside . . . .' The old man's leathery lips shut like a trap as he dully realized he had said too much.

'Gold, huh. Out here? You must ha' been lucky, old-timer!' Kurt stared at the canvas bag tied to the burro, near to the dirty, tattered saddle-bag that hung there, too.

'Mind your own bisness, mister. I ain't got no gold. What makes yuh figure I got gold? Ain't no gold for miles around – jest rock an' sand an' rattlers. Plenty of rattlers.' The oldster's whiskery face seemed to twitch in anger. His torn pants were tied to his hips with some old manila rope and his checked shirt bore signs of many dubious meals. His boots were scuffed and far too big for his feet although they had been expensive hand-made items at some time in the past. He carried an old Colt in a yellow leather holster that had been often stitched together. In a sudden crazy fury he took off his shapeless old hat and whipped it against his legs a number of times. Apparently this was his way of demonstrating his swift old anger! Kurt Kallon grinned at the old man.

'What are you going to do about the burro, oldster?'

'I ain't so old. I jest look old – on account of the hard life I've had.'

Kallon brought out his fast-draw single-action Peacemaker 'Best to put that old burro out of its misery, mister. Are you going to do it or will you leave it to me?'

'You can do it,' said the old man cunningly. 'An' then yuh can give me a ride into town.'

Grimly, Kurt pointed his gun at the dying beast and triggered. The noise of the gun echoed for miles around as the burro gave its last twitch.

The oldster looked on admiringly at the 44-40 Peacemaker and put out a hand. 'Kin I get the feel of that hogleg? Sure is a mighty fine piece of artillery.'

With a thin grin on his unshaven face, Kurt handed over the weapon and the oldster balanced the gun in his hand. Then with a twist to his wind- and sun-battered face, the old man jerked the gun around and pointed it at Kurt Kallon.

'I could kill yuh – take your hoss an' saddle-bags an' ride to hell out of it! You made a mistake, mister!'

'No – you've made the mistake.' Kurt lunged like a flash of lightning, grabbing at the gun and pushing the small saddle-tramp to one side. At the same time his arms went around the cunning oldster, forcing his neck back grimly. The old man gave a choking yell, revealing his yellow teeth, and his fingers tried to prise away Kurt's grip.

'No use, oldster. I'm a wrestler – fought with Mountain Man and Gorilla. Know them?'

'Jeeze, I'm – agh – choking! Never heard of 'em!'

'Best in the business – an' I beat 'em fair an' square. Now what the hell am I goin' to do with you? Cain't leave you out here miles from anywhere.'

'You gotta take me into town. Double up! That big hoss of yourn can take us easy. Aw, ease off, mister. You're choking me! I didn't mean any harm. I'll – I'll – give you some gold!'

'I could take it – the lot. You figured you could trick me, old man. My name is Kurt Kallon an' I don't like tricks. Now what's your label?'

'Aw, hell – I'm Dad Bowker – jest an old galoot who means no harm.'

'Dad? I bet you ain't no Dad! If you are, God help the litle brats.'

'Jest a nickname they gave me long ways back. Now, hell, let's get outa here.'

Kurt took long strides back to his horse and threw a mocking glance at the other man. 'You can get up behind me and don't even try to pull a trick on me again. I might break your scrawny neck.'

Dad Bowker was sufficiently agile to be able to swing up to Kurt's saddle and position himself comfortably behind him. The big-boned animal took a few strides forward and then, with Dad Bowker and his bags nicely balanced, they went down the sandy gully.

All at once, it seemed, a man, a horse and a gun appeared on the ridge. The new gun pointed menacingly at Kurt and the oldster.

'I heard a shot. What's going on, Dad? Seems you got a new sidekick. Big feller, huh?'

As Kurt reined in and stared at this fat old rider and the pointed gun, he figured he got the picture.

'You two buzzards know each other?'

'We was pards – an' he's got my share of the gold!' The fat man's voice was full of snarled anger. 'He rode off, the twisty little saddle-bug! Got my gold!'

'Hell, you killed the old prospector to get it!' Dad Bowker retaliated.

Kurt stared again. 'Nice pair, ain't yuh! Let's see if I got it right. You both helped kill some prospector an' took his gold. Then Dad here goes off with the poke of gold. Is that it?'

'About right, feller,' mocked the fat man, sitting his

Deadly Gold

horse comfortably. 'But I got the gun covering you two an' I want the gold. So one of you unhook that canvas poke an' drop it nice and easy to the ground and then hit the breeze.'

The man was round-bellied, as dirty as Dad Bowker and grey-bearded. His mount was a sullen brute with no spirit. The man wore a flannel shirt that had been slept in, it seemed, for weeks, and his pants were tweed stretched tight over fat thighs. He was as grubby as his pal, Dad Bowker.

'I don't like third-rate crap telling me what to do,' said Kurt slowly.

'I got the drop on yuh!'

'You figure wrong, fat man.'

Kurt's Peacemaker was the fast-draw model and Kurt suddenly proved the fact. He whipped the gun from leather with a blur of hand-motion and fired at the fat man's pointed gun in the same fraction of a second. The loosely-held weapon flew to the earth as Kurt's slug impacted on metal. The fatso gave a howl of fright and pain and jerked his numbed hand back. His gun was deep in dusty sand. The man put his hand under his armpit like a caned schoolboy and howled.

The tableau held for some drawn-out seconds, while Kurt grinned and waited until the wisp of smoke cleared from his gun, The horses steadied. Dad Bowker yelled: 'Go ahead – kill the bastard! You got him good an' proper!'

'You want to hang on to this gold, huh?' Kurt snapped to the man behind him. 'Damned if I haven't run into a right pair of snakes!'

'Kill him! I'll share the gold with you! Yeah – stick a slug in his fat gut.'

'This gold is going to the sheriff in Cragside.' Kurt

twisted in his saddle and rammed his gun into Dad Bowker's skinny ribs. 'Got any objections?'

'I tell you it's my gold!'

'I figure you can get mighty tiring, Dad!' Kurt turned again. He yelled to the fat man who contrived to glare and control his mount at the same time. 'I'm ridin' for Cragside. I figure it's best if you stay ahead of me.'

'What in hell for?'

'When we hit town you two can talk to the lawman there – see if you can convince him who owns this gold.'

Kurt figured it was time he relieved Dad Bowker of his ancient gun, so he whipped a hand around and lifted the Colt from the yellow holster.

'Hey! What in hell!'

'I don't feel happy with an old snake behind me sporting an old smokepole. You know somethin', Dad?'

'What?'

'Reckon I'd sooner trust a sidewinder than you two prize buzzards. Now let's get goin'. That damned sun is sinking.'

He had to get back to his partners. They were the kind who actually worried about him, typical of their nature. Kurt chuckled. Thinking about his two side-kicks, he realized he should never have left them to venture out on their own. They'd sure as heck get into some tight spot, being the species they were.

'Have you got a name, shit?' he called out to the man riding just ahead.

'He's a bastard name o' Snap,' yelled Dad Bowker.

'Is that a name? Snap what?'

'Just Snap,' growled the man ahead. 'An' what's it to you, mister? Just give Dad an' me our gold and we'll ride on.'

'So you can try an' kill each other, huh? Well, you ain't got guns – but that never stopped men from salivating each other. Nope. I reckon the law should know about this gold. Now just lengthen the stride of that old nag, feller, and we'll get to town a bit quicker. I got my pards to meet.'

'Pards?' chuckled Dad Bowker. 'So you're not a loner?'

'Never get the chance to be alone.'

'I bet them pards of yourn are tough cusses like you!'

Kurt laughed. 'They're plenty tough when it's needed . . . .'

'Pack guns, huh?'

'Yeah, they can handle hardware. Any more questions, old-timer?'

'I ain't old – I told yuh! Maybe I'll meet your two pards, mister. Maybe they'll like gold better than you.'

'Maybe – but not stolen gold with a dead prospector behind it.'

Kurt made the man called Snap jig his animal along just a shade faster and the hills behind Cragside slowly took more shape as they put the miles behind them. Snap's horse was old and couldn't be hurried.

The two were a darned nuisance but Kurt figured the law could handle them. He realized his old experiences as a badge-packer still clung to him, the old respect for law and order in a frontier land where law got a bit blurred.

Kurt knew the man called Snap was a rogue and Dad Bowker not much better and he cursed the pair of them for getting in his way. But the gold was the problem. He could drop the two old villains the moment he hit the rock-girt town but the poke of gold had to be dealt with. Seemed the best he could do would be to lodge it with the sheriff, get a receipt for it and try to forget the gold and the two range-hardened oldsters. Seeing his two partners again was a more attractive idea than fooling with Dad Bowker and Snap.

Snap's mount slowed them. The trail back was reduced to a snail's pace. Kurt made sure the man was always ahead. One thing was for certain, he couldn't gallop off.

Dad made another try. 'Gold, huh! Don't you like gold, big man? Don't you want some of it?'

'I'll take it to the lawman in Cragside – as I've told you.'

'That's a fool idea.'

Kurt laughed grimly. 'You afraid the sheriff might want to know how the prospector died?'

'He jest got careless . . . .'

'You mean unlucky enough to meet up with you two!'

'You figure to tell the sheriff we kilt the prospector,' snarled Snap, his double chin like a balloon of flesh. 'I'll say you're a blamed liar, anyway. You ever met up with that sheriff in Cragside?'

'Nope. Can't say I've had the pleasure.'

'Name of Carl Rigg. We met up once . . . .'

'That figures,' laughed Kurt. 'What did you do?'

'Jest a misunderstanding, mister. I tell you that *hombre* is one hard man . . . .'

'He's a sheriff. Guess he's got to be tough dealing with villains.'

'He's a twister, feller. More a bastard than a lawman.'

'Well, you would say that, Snap, old man.' Kurt shook his head in some sort of disbelief in the other's words.

'He's a crook!' yelled Snap.

'And you're an honest galoot, huh?' Kurt stared ahead at the fading light.

He thought the pace of the animals was too slow. Kurt jigged his mount up to the crowbait Snap was riding and rapped the animal across the haunches.

'Giddup! We ain't got all day!'

Fatso Snap took the hint and kept his horse moving fast. As a pair the animals went on a bit quicker. In this way they proceeded swiftly enough and got to town just as the street lanterns were being lit by the old man paid to wander around the town and light the wicks.

Gold or no gold, Kurt felt he had to find his two volatile young partners, just to check they were not in trouble. It was in their nature, and indeed their appearances, that conflict found root. Being the kind they were, sure as hell some fool would start a play with them.

He rode around a tall rooming-house with the two disgruntled old villains close to him. Kurt stared at the veranda and the numerous windows hoping to sight his partners. But of course they weren't around. That figured. He knew he couldn't trust them! They should be in the rooms he had got for them but maybe that was asking too much.

'Aw, the hell!' he yelled. 'We'll go see the sheriff an' get this gold dealt with! And you two!'

'I don't care much for the law,' growled Dad Bowker.

'You don't say! You do surprise me, Dad!'

'That sheriff is a tricky cuss,' warned Snap. 'I've told you! I've heard things about him. Sure surprised you don't know the man better.'

'I don't mix much with sheriffs these days, old fatso man.'

Kurt figured the two old range-roamers were trying to avoid a showdown because of the dubious way they had obtained the gold. Well, that was for the sheriff to decide. For himself, he wanted out of this situation. He'd hand the gold and the thieves to the law and let them deal with it.

The sheriff and his deputy were inside the wooden office, apparently having a powwow. Kurt barged in hauling Dad and Snap with him – and the poke of gold.

'Two villains and gold!' he rapped, and he started to explain. When Kurt put the canvas poke on the desk he did see the gleam in Sheriff Carl Rigg's eyes. The man was a thick-set gentleman with a large handlebar moustache. He had an air of authority and a badge to back it up but Kurt did not like him right from the start. The authority sat like a bullying mantle on the man. His deputy was the tall lean type and pretty much the same age as Carl Rigg, and Kurt figured both men had seen everything in their time. Still, they had been elected by the town councillors and had to be trusted.

'Leave the gold. I'll put it in the safe.' Rigg moved towards the hefty iron box which bore the name of some manufacturer in the East and had probably been brought in when the railroad first reached Fort Worth.

'Guess I need a receipt,' muttered Kurt.

'Yeah? Waal, why not?' Carl Rigg's eyes gleamed craftily. 'We do things right around here in Cragside, mister. And nice to meet a man who has respect for the law.'

'What about these two villains? I figure they killed to get this gold.'

'You're a liar!' snarled Dad Bowker.

Snap began shaking his fist at Kurt, at which point

the deputy grabbed the fat oldster. 'Guess we'll stick these two in the cells, Mr Rigg, huh?'

'Yeah. Cool 'em off!' The solution was easily reached, too easily, Kurt thought. But what could he do? He picked up the paper receipt and then with a sudden sure-fire hunch he tore the slip in two, grabbed at the canvas poke of gold and backed off, gun in hand.

'I don't trust you two gents. I'll see the law in Fort Worth!'

'Hey! You can't do that! We're the law! We'll deal with this!'

'Yeah. I'll get the law to settle this in Fort Worth, with gents I can trust.'

'Why, you bastard, I'm the sheriff in Cragside! Put that hogleg back in leather! Put that poke o' gold back on my desk!'

Kurt held his gun very steady and to the two so-called lawmen it seemed like a small cannon and the man behind it a cuss who had triggered many times. They glared, the deputy and the sheriff, itching to touch their own guns but knowing with certainty that was a dangerous game. Snap and Dad Bowker moved slightly away in the small office apprehension in their wary old eyes. They weren't quite sure which way this play was going but at least they were not behind bars!

'Let's git,' snapped Kurt. 'We'll ride on to Fort Worth tomorrow.'

'You're stealin' that gold!' snarled Carl Rigg.

'Don't give me horse-crap!' Kurt backed to the door, pushing Dad Bowker and Snap with him. 'I've got these two old villains to back up my story. I guess I'll have to trust to the law in Fort Worth – when I get there – an' that won't be tonight.'

Carl Rigg pointed a finger at Kurt. 'I'll ride to Fort

Worth, too. You don't trick me, mister. As a sheriff, my word will carry more weight than yourn.'

'This gold is tempting you, huh?' Kurt opened the door leading to the boardwalk and street. He gave Dad Bowker and Snap another push. 'Let's hit the road. You two can go free. I'll hand this gold in at Fort Worth and the hell with it! Vamoose you two old villains!'

'You hangin' on to that gold, damn yuh, mister?'

'Yeah – an' I want to see my two pretty pards!'

TWO

It wasn't easy to get rid of the two old villains. They stood at the door of the big rooming house and argued with Kurt Kallon about gold and the reasons why they were damned sure they were entitled to it. In the end Kurt almost threw them out on the boardwalk as he slammed the door of the old wooden structure. He had to find his newly acquired partners – God only knew why because he hardly owed them any allegiance, and in some ways they were a nuisance, although mighty pretty with it!

He had to get back to his main quest and that was to find the three lousy rats who had killed Billy Graham, now dead and buried out in the wastelands. Billy had been a special young sidekick, although Kurt hadn't known him very long. Billy had known the two girls, taken them to dances at the mission hall and they'd all been pals for a few intensive weeks.

Kurt Kallon's partners were, in truth, two lovely young girls. It seemed they had been wished upon him by circumstances, the way they had all met and enjoyed a sudden friendship. And now there were just the two girls, Charity and Rose, and it seemed to Kurt that he couldn't just ride away and leave them to fend

19

for themselves, because Billy Graham had been like a brother to them all.

The night was late. He had to find his partners. Surely by now they were in their rooms. So independent and wilful, they had been out in the town on their own, sure they could look after themselves. And they could, packing guns. Rose Merit and Charity Brendan had the guts of young men but they were without any doubt two lovely young girls and provocative with it.

'What have you two been up to?' he asked when he found them.

'Nothing much. Just chasing off horny galoots like yourself!' Rose gave him another impulsive kiss, the result of which confirmed her recent description of him. 'But Charity here has gotten herself a new man. You see you shouldn't leave us gals alone in a town like this.'

'I haven't got this man, as you put it,' snapped Charity. 'He has simply got it into his big head to chase me. I guess he figures I'm easy.'

'Well, you are!' shrilled Rose.

'No more than you, hot pants!' Charity always had a swift answer for her friend.

The girls were not dressed in the conventional clothes which the other women in Cragside adopted, but preferred jeans, blue denim material, usually the choice of working cow-hands and the stable-men in the town. The two girls stretched the pants provocatively, something the staid women in town objected to because their men seemed to be fascinated by the shapes of Charity and Rose.

Also the girls wore blouses which really did dip and reveal a lot of globular flesh, something else that grabbed the attention of the men of Cragside.

And the women in town, with their long dresses did not wear gun-belts and holsters and display heavy Colts in the leather, something that Rose and Charity took for granted. They had needed to use those guns at various times in the past.

But the thing that really enraged the other women in the cow-town, and startled all the passing men, was the use of some kind of lip reddener, the stuff used by the whores in the saloons. But Rose and Charity were not loose women, as some guys discovered when a gun was stuck in their ribs, or even lower down in their body structure. The girls just figured that all life should be fun and they liked the look of their red lips in a mirror. If men wanted to kiss them, wasn't that fun, too?

'I'll take a look at this guy of yourn, Charity,' warned Kurt.

'I've told you more than once, Kurt, I don't need a chaperone.'

He grinned and changed the subject. 'I'll have to guard this gold. Already too many pesky rogues want to lay their hands on it. We'll have to ride to Fort Worth. Then we hit the trail for those dirty killers – three bastards who've got to end up dead.'

'So we'll have to start first thing come sun-up,' commented Rose. 'That means we got to get our heads down pretty soon.'

Kurt nodded and took off his gun-belt. 'Guess I'll have to sluice off some of this trail dust. But I'll have to get Big Feller a stall somewhere and that means going out into the night and unhitching him from that tie rail. Will you two gals be all right for some minutes iffen I have to leave you again?'

'Guess we can live without you,' mocked Charity.

He grinned. 'Sure? You don't always talk like that.'

'Gawd – you figure we've got hot pants for you all the time? Now I tell you, Kurt, my darling, there is this other man out there. Maybe you'll meet him.'

'Maybe I'll land him one – if I don't like him.'

'You don't own me!' yelled Charity.

'Nor me!' added Rose with a taunting look.

His grin continued to decorate his firm lips, an indication that he could remember the times when he had held the girls in his arms, but not simultaneously. He had enjoyed moments with Rose and Charity, when they had been in the mood to play along and he was out of the saddle and had free time.

'Now who in the heck would want to own you two she-cats!' He went to the room door. 'I got to see to me hoss. Some things come first in a man's life.'

'Yeah?' shouted Rose. "Wal, men don't always come first with this lady!'

'Lady? What lady?' Kurt had to leave when Rose came rushing towards him. He shut the door on her.

He was still grinning when he got to the street and felt the hard-packed dirt crunch under his boots. Patting his gun-belt he realized he had left his 44-40 Peacemaker with the girls in the bedroom. Well, that didn't matter. He lunged towards the tie rail and his horse – and then halted abruptly when two hefty men strode grimly towards him. The sheriff and his side-kick!

The dark street was full of shadows but the real menace was in the shape of these two men.

'Where's the gold, feller?' Carl Rigg was tough in speech and manner.

'I ain't got it on me, that's for sure. Too bad, huh?'

The two greedy so-called lawmen were not in the

mood for trading snappy remarks.

'Git him!'

Two sets of arms flung out at Kurt, with four bunched fists thudding at him. The first blows met thin air because Kurt had been in bouts like this in his past, but suddenly Carl Rigg rammed in a punch that jolted Kurt. As he staggered back a bit, the tall lean deputy got behind Kurt, grabbed an arm and began twisting it behind Kurt's body. Carl Rigg rammed in another two punches, rage at not finding the gold lending him strength. Blood appeared on Kurt's split lip. He spat out the warm stuff and whipped a fist at the rogue sheriff, which connected and gave that gent something to think about. Carl Rigg blinked as his eyesight hazed. Despite the deputy trying to hold his arms, Kurt flung off the grip and shot off another punch that banged into the sheriff's optics once again. At the same time Kurt kicked backwards with one big boot and gave the deputy a thud on his shin which made him howl.

But two angry hell-bents were a lot to handle. Carl Rigg abandoned fisticuffs and kicked low at Kurt's body, right between the legs, and like any man Kurt felt the breath-taking anguish. He involuntarily doubled over. Carl Rigg landed another punch which broke skin on Kurt's cheek and made blood paint his face.

Kurt Kallon forced the nausea out of his guts, got his fists flailing again and had the satisfaction of hitting the sheriff really hard on the nose. Kurt kicked backwards again and nearly broke the tall deputy's leg as boot jarred into bone. The man backed and limped. Kurt closed with Carl Rigg and slammed a right and a left into the man's guts, just hard enough to hurt like hell. The sheriff's snarled groan was proof that he had been hit really bad. Kurt gave no mercy. He rammed more punches and as the sheriff crumpled to the earth, Kurt hauled him up by his gun-belt and slammed a finisher to the man's jaw. That punch hurt Kurt's knuckles but he got joy out of it all the same.

Still, even Kurt Kallon was breathing heavily and swaying on firmly planted boots in the dust. And then two lithe smaller figures rushed out of the doorway behind him and screamed, as was their nature.

'Kurt – are you all right?'

'You've got blood on your face!'

And then Charity and Rose began to kick at the prone sheriff. At this display of female ferocity, the tall thin deputy figured retreat was the best answer, although he was armed.

'Leave him,' advised Kurt. 'This galoot is the legal sheriff of this town.'

'I figure we're in bad,' murmured Rose. 'How long in jail do we get for kicking a lawman where it hurts?'

'Don't worry,' jerked Kurt. 'We're headin' out for Fort Worth come sun-up, where we might get some intelligent interest in this gold. Aw, hell – I want to get Big Feller into a stable for the night an' then we'll sleep. Gee – that's somethin' I need!'

They didn't realize that just around the corner of a timber building the two scallywags, Dad Bowker and Snap, had watched the fight and the shouted remarks with interest.

'Taking that damned gold to Fort Worth,' snarled Dad Bowker. His leathery lips twisted. 'Well the hell with that hefty bastard! We'll still git that gold back!'

Snap noted he was included in the crafty oldster's remarks. That suited him. Gold was a substance that could easily be moved from one man to another, especially if one gent was dead!

The night air was becoming increasingly colder and the two old villains beat a retreat to a nearby saloon where there was oil-lamp light, drink and grub and time to yap over plans to retrieve the gold.

As for Kurt Kallon, he got back to the girls when Big Feller had been safely placed in the capable hands of an old hostler. Charity began to apply cold water to a bloodied bruise on Kurt's cheek.

'Did they really hurt you?'

'I'm a wrestler, remember.' He smiled. 'Let's get some sleep.'

'When the hell are we goin' to ride after them damned killers?' Rose Merit demanded. She ran her long fingers through her red hair and looked cross. 'We seem to be foolin' around a lot. The trail will be stone cold. Just how do you plan to get back to tracking them down, Kurt?'

He sat down and nodded. 'We know something about them. They killed Billy because he bested them at a card game in that damned saloon and then they took the winnings. So they are gamblers – and cowards – murderous cowards with guns. Three bastards. We got a description of them from other rannigans in the saloon.'

Rose nodded. 'Hard riders! Wanderers who ride from town to town, ranch to ranch and from job to job – when they have to work for a living.'

Kurt nodded. 'One was a 'breed, we were told. No damned names – but that means nothing because I figure as law-breakers they'd have plenty of names. And one of the three was in his late forties, some sort of hard-case with two flashy guns, we were told.'

'Yeah – and the third was some sort of beardless kid. We know all this from the talks we had in the saloon. How on earth are we gonna find them, Kurt? Where can they be?'

'In the damned badlands beyond Fort Worth by now I reckon. Could be they'll head for Casino Tent. I reckon you two gals ain't heard of that place.' He grinned. 'Truth is, I haven't hit that third-rate dump myself in my travels. It's a tent-town – only sprung up since the snows faded away. God knows where they got the gear. Must ha' come up on wagons from heaven knows where.'

'Just what is Casino Tent?' asked Charity.

'What the name implies, my dear. A big tent run by some gambling gent, with no law except by use of Colt-fire. Money talks in a joint like that – and the losers are very often dead men a few hours later. Even the winners have to really look after their own skins. That's where our three killer swines will be, intent on winning more money.'

'And what if they lose?'

'Gamblers never figure on losing.'

'And if they did they'd get out fast,' added Rose.

'And what if these three murderers are not in this Casino Tent place?'

'Then we'll have to keep on riding.'

'Tracking around.' Rose yawned. 'I'm tired.'

The two girls were in the bed they shared in the other room about ten minutes later, and Kurt Kallon got his head down in the second bedroom, wearing nothing, heat radiating from his hard lean body and contained in the single blanket that covered him. He seemed to sleep instantly. And then he was gently nudged into a drowsy awareness of another body beside him. He knew by the womanly scent that this was Charity, her blonde hair always retaining that alluring odour even after hours of riding. Yeah, Charity!

'What d'you want?' As if he didn't know what this sexy bitch always wanted of a man.

'Be nice to me, Kurt.'

'Ain't yuh tired, gal?'

'Sure – but I'd like to be loved.'

Smiling, he considered this an enticing request. She wore only a thin cotton slip, clean and smelling of woman.

'Is Rose asleep?'

'Sure thing. Anyway, Rose doesn't own you.'

'Nope. I'm my own man.'

'Except when you belong to us.' Her hands began caressing his lean naked body, with mutual warmth permeating their flesh, a process which made Kurt groan, not that her fingers caused him pain. His mumbled sounds, audible only to the girl, were more sensual in nature than anything else. He began to undulate his body in the age-old manner of the male inflamed by a lovely woman. His trail-weary flesh responded to the soft, skilful stimuli of the girl and for some time they wrestled – and this was a bout which caused Kurt no pain.

When she had left, he fell asleep and dreamed strangely of ugly gunnies and horses on long trails. then he became aware of another lithe body sliding close to his naked skin. He knew this was Rose and for some crazy moments he realized two women could be one too many. All the same he put his arms around her. For a man like Kurt Kallon defeat in any way was not on.

THREE

They rested at the top of the grassy rise, three men of differing stature and needs, character and ages. The sun was ready to sink. The air was still and chilly. Their horses were ground-hitched behind them with ample grass to crop. The riders had eaten in silence, being men who knew when to shut up and when to yap. Their saddle-bags and other gear were behind them, serving as backrests for men who were hard of muscle but nevertheless human beings who could tire. One man, the 'breed in dirty tweed pants and a red checked shirt, slowly pointed down the hill at the cluster of tents around the creek.

'When the hell are we gonna get a crack at winnin' some real *dinero*?' His aquiline features were always set in a bitter mould.

'When the games get started. Them players have rode in with money. Better to let it git circulated, huh?' The man inched his backside along the hard grass, his twin Colts sagging heavily in the supple holsters. Hec Redman wore his prize guns when asleep, at least that was the way it seemed to his partners in ruffianly crime. Sure, he did unhitch his gun-belt at times, only

29

when he went with a saloon woman or took a bath, the latter procedure being infrequent.

'You like to boss us galoots!' sneered the 'breed. He had a curious lisp and a high voice which some fool men had taken for weakness in the past. These gents were now dead.

'Some bastard has to figure things out,' rasped Hec Redman. 'I like to tell others what to do – not take orders.'

'One day I won't take orders from the likes o' you!' snapped back the 'breed known as Harry. That name had sufficed for him in a dozen cow-towns and with many partners.

'Then you'll end up corpsed!' the older man with the twin hardware rapped back with antagonism. These three men were never partners in friendship.

The young man with them stared with unlined, unshaven face. He was holding his Colt, balancing it with nervy fingers. He was a twitchy young fellow, never resting, except when he needed to sleep, and then he was out, unconscious, so far in a pit of slumber that the others had to shake him to get him back to life.

'I'd like to git down to that casino and pick up some easy money. I mean, that dough we got off that gink we corpsed won't last for ever.'

'I never said it was enough,' sneered Hec Redman. He leered with a twisted glance at the young Kid Curtis. He really despised the young gunny, mainly because of the age difference, although they had the same skills with guns, hand-guns or long smoke-pole.

'So we'll ride down – git a drink – play some cards!' Kid Curtis rapped nervily. His speech was always staccato.

'We will do jest that,' sneered the older man. 'Hope you are lucky, pal!'

'I'm good with a gun – an' that's all that matters.' Kid Curtis shoved his hat back on his mop of tousled fair hair.

They had eaten beans and bacon, cooked on their camp-fire, and drank their bitter black coffee. The land around was hostile, with a fair amount of grass for the animals but hard on a man's back and backside and the horizon so many miles distant only served to remind these men that they were just dots in a vast land. Strangely, the tent town, a mile away down the sloping land, was a kind of consolation, a reminder that other men – and maybe women – shared this wide empty land.

The sun sank swiftly when the time arrived. The three men saddled their mounts again, tightened the leathers on the lean rangy animals, They touched their guns, a habit they had, like all men who needed the metal hardware to survive. They drank the dregs of their coffee and spat out the taste in disgust. They pulled down their hats and got onto the saddles, inching a slow way down the slope, each man with his own grim thoughts.

Three killers! In their lives a dead man was just a nuisance. Sometimes they had to bury them!

Silently, they let the horses pick a way down the uneven grassy slope and with every few yards the collection of tents became more defined, with the big canvas in the centre. An enterprising gent had brought the big tent all the way from Fort Worth in the sure knowledge that the law would stick to the town and leave this settlement of gunnies and card-players to their own way of life. The big tent boasted more than cards. The enter-

prising gent had brought a roulette wheel along, bought
when a similar joint had collapsed after the owner
stopped a slug from a Remington carbine.

The three men hitched the animals and cautiously
moved into the tent, yellow oil-light meeting their eyes
and revealing a cluster of tables and two bar counters
for the convenience of the many wandering riders who
had come in for the night. An old man squeezed a
battered concertina and wheezed out some wailing
Irish tunes. He sat in a corner and stashed a big mug
of ale at his feet.

Hec Redman surveyed the joint, his black hat down
over his eyes.

'There's real money here,' he muttered.

'Where'n hell does it come from – out here in the
wilds?' Harry wanted to know.

'Same sort of jaspers as us,' sneered the older man.
'I bet every goddamned dollar here has been lifted from
someone else.'

He knew the gamblers at the tables and those
standing at the bars were undoubtedly gunnies and
wanted men, every man jack of them. Casino Tent was
a haven for their kind. No sheriff in his right mind
would want to visit the place; few honest men like
ranchers and storekeepers from Fort Worth would
want to ride into the joint. It was for hell-bents and the
kind of gambling man who figured he could take real
chances.

'I wanna drink,' snapped Kid Curtis.

'Keep your mouth buttoned!' snapped Hec Redman.

'Tellin' me what to do again?'

'Some gink has to keep a young fool like you in
control. Sure – git a drink – but don't talk about the
money an' how we got it.'

'That third-rate cuss is dead!'

'Sure, an' you helped kill him. You pumped slugs into him even after he fell.'

'An' you fired the first slug!'

The two men, so different in age and physique, swapped sneering glances and then sidled up to the bar, which consisted of long thick planks placed on big barrels. With antagonistic stares at the bartender they got their drinks, three glasses of rotgut whiskey out of a new bottle. They made sure the bottle was placed before them on the plank bar. Then they drank greedily and replenished, all in minutes.

'We'll pick up some easy *dinero* here!' Kid Curtis jerked eagerly, glancing around. 'Look at the gold and bills on some of the tables. Easy, I reckon. Let's git started.'

His young enthusiasm was dampened when they discovered a man had to pay for the hire of a table.

'Six dollars!' he rasped to the bulky man who held a Colt with one hand and collected fees with the other. The big bearded specimen grinned and pointed his hardware at Kid Curtis.

'This ain't no free show. You want to sit in with other card men, you pay them, too.'

Hec Redman twisted his lips and pushed his hat back on his head. It was noticeable that his hair was thinning.

'We'll sit in with others. We ain't takin' money off each other, not us three. We want to play with the big money, huh!'

So they sat in with other gamblers eventually, taking their drinks with them. Hec Redman knew there wasn't an unarmed rannigan in the tent. With the tensions of winning or losing money, the rotgut drink and the hardware, it was easy to figure that some of the hard cusses would be dead meat before the night was done, killed by their fellow gamblers, with not a law-badge in sight. There wasn't even an undertaker in Casino Tent. Dead men were just slung out on the wastelands. Eventually they were just bones. They shared this fate with horses and any other animal that just dropped dead.

Hec Redman sat in with three rangemen who were just a bit too drunk to handle their cards expertly and so he began to win, playing craftily and staying almost sober. Harry, the 'breed, played carefully like his partner at another table. One of the gentlemen he had sat in with didn't care for 'breeds and made it plain with muttered comments every time he put a grubby card on the table or put out money. Harry watched him, hated him and continued to use his hand of cards with skill and to pick up *dinero*. Kid Curtis, on the other hand, was unlucky from the start with two other players. He wasn't a good man with a deck of cards. He seemed to dislike his jacks and had a complete lack of aces. He was losing money. It was dead man's money but that was of no account.

One of the Kid's opponents was a little man in dirty gear which suggested he had punched cows for some time but now had enough money and luck to gamble. He was taking cash from Kid Curtis.

The Kid pushed back his chair. The grating sound made others look up. The earth was hard-baked and the chairs hefty and rough; they made plenty of noise when moved.

'You got all the aces in the goddammed pack, huh?' The Kid's challenge rasped out.

'Just the luck of the game!' The little man had a

squeaky voice. Kid Curtis figured to despise him right from the start. Instead of being easy meat, the runty man was damned good with his hand.

'Luck – shit!'

'I ain't cheating!'

'Yeah? I ain't in the habit of bein' licked!'

Kid Curtis noted the little man wore a gun but the hardware seemed as big as him. The little man just didn't seem to be the gunny type. Kid Curtis was on his feet. He glared down at the table, at the little man, the money and the cards. Impulsive as ever, thinking hardly being part of his young brain, he swept a fast hand over the bills on the table and managed to grab most of them. He backed, his gun in his hand. It seemed to be a small cannon.

'Hey, you can't do this!' the small man spluttered.

'The hell with yuh!' Kid Curtis backed another foot, his gun plumb steady on the little guy and ready to swivel to the other gambler if he looked ready to grab at hardware. The Kid held on tightly to the fistful of dollar bills. A few yards away, Hec Redman noted this play with thinned lips. He tensed. Harry stiffened and muttered some strange Indian curses.

'That's my cash!' The small man rose swiftly, clawing for his gun. Kid Curtis reckoned he was easy meat. The Kid had the money and his own gun was clear of leather. He thought the little galoot had no chance.

But the Kid had consumed too much rotgut in too short a time, and fast as all hell it seemed the small man triggered with surprising skill. The Colt boomed out the deadly slug, stopping gambling all around. The small man crouched, glaring, the smoke from his gun wisping into the tent air and mingling with the other stinks from cigars and the like.

As for Kid Curtis, he staggered back, fell over his chair and thudded to the hard ground, yelling his pain for all to hear. 'Aw – goddamn – yuh got me – aw – hell it hurts!'

'You won't die,' said the little man calmly.

For all his composure and speed with his gun, he still wasn't fast enough to master the situation completely. As Kid Curtis fell, Hec Redman and Harry acted. Swiftly, acting in circumstances that had happened to them in previous situations, they grabbed at the cash on the tables and backed, guns in hands.

They knew that for the moment they would survive if they stuck together. If they didn't help each other, they'd go down. They were surrounded by ruffians.

Kid Curtis staggered to his feet and crazily grabbed at the money again, leaving traces of his blood all over the place. He backed, instinctively joining his pals.

'Let's git!' he yelled with his youthful bravado. His shoulder was tearing pain into his flesh where the slug had lodged. But he could still move quickly.

'Damned fool!' snarled Hec Redman and joined his companions, gun in hand, dominating the scene, or so it seemed with Harry and his menacing hardware. They clutched at money as if it was more important than life itself. They backed, with the Kid moaning as the hurt began to sear through him.

The big guy who had taken money for the rent of gaming tables figured he could control things because this was his job in the tent and he had a gun in his hand. He yelled a warning to Hec Redman and the two others, a fool thing to do.

Harry whipped his well-used gun around instantly and fired at the bearded individual, a shot aimed directly at the wide, barrelled chest. The bark of the

gun sent gamblers plunging for the earth floor. The
bearded man sank slowly, his red lips parted as he
gasped for breath and pressed a hand to the blood
pumping from his chest and felt the strength flood out
of his thick legs.

'Arrggh!' His strangled roar was a mad thing. He
was dying. He fell on all fours and tried to move like a
wounded animal, leaving blood on the hard earth floor.
No man came to his aid. He sank again while the grim
gamblers watched him die. They didn't give a damn for
him. He was one more brute breathing his last.

As for Hec Redman and Harry, they were backing to
the tent entrance. Kid Curtis was trying desperately to
follow them, his legs momentarily weak. He scrambled
on to his feet and swayed, his young face twisted in
anger and pain, his gun still clamped by a sweaty
hand. Instinctively, he backed to join his two partners,
blundering past chairs and tables.

The little man with the squeaky voice scowled and
his gun followed the three hardcases. The Kid was
bleeding badly from his shoulder wound but this agony
did not prevent him from chasing around to join his
pals. The three had protection in numbers it seemed,
and the benefit of some surprise, but all the same other
grim men in the tent were touching gun butts. So far
only Harry, the 'breed, had fired a shot. But the little
man had cause to go for his gun.

He brought the big Colt around again with the inten-
tion of firing at Kid Curtis and stopping him in his
tracks and so retrieving his cash, but he had reckoned
without Harry's black, beady eyes. The 'breed jerked his
gun and fired, a shattered second in time that also
obliterated the little gambler for all eternity. Harry's
slug cut smoky air and blasted into the runty guy.

Two down! Harry, the 'breed, was excelling himself!

Many gamblers were cowering, seeking some sort of safety near the tables. A few itched to shoot the three retreating men but held back. So the three thugs who had killed Billy, among others in their lives, were getting away with the reckless gun-play.

Men yelled. 'Goddamn! Damn them!'

'We want to play cards!' one jasper snarled plaintively.

'Aw, shit – cain't a man have a drink in peace!'

Hec Redman, Harry and Kid Curtis were at the tent entrance, where the night air blew in refreshingly. They moved slowly.

They knew the horses were out there. The only safety lay in getting to hell away from the tent and the angry gamblers. Just one random shot might ruin everything.

The three men still clutched at dollar bills; some of them were of high denominations. They needed to get away with the money – and their lives!

The money the three hardcases held was a bit higher than the sum with which they had walked into Casino Tent, but was not exactly a fortune. They had taken a lot of risks for not a lot of *dinero*.

As the three got to their horses, backsides hitting leather, some men in the tent loosed off some shots, most of which simply tore holes in the tent. And then with a dust-raising scurry of hooves, the three were high-tailing down the beaten trail leading out of the place.

'Goddamn – you lost us the chance to pick up money!' yelled Hec Redman above the ratapan of hoof-beats.

'Who? Me?' spat Kid Curtis. 'Weren't me! Damn yuh,

Redman! Harry kilt that bearded big gink!'

'We could ha' made some easy spending money.' Hec Redman always assumed his wisdom was superior to the others.

'We got some bills—'

'Just hoss-shit!'

They were out in the grasslands now and could afford to slacken the pace of the animals. It was then that Kid Curtis fell slowly from his mount and rolled over and over on the earth before coming to rest in a motionless huddle.

FOUR

The three horses were plodding on, taking the trail to Fort Worth. The track was well defined for some miles after it left Cragside, even among the broken lands where gullies and rocky outcrops were numerous. Eventually it led on to the plain, where the grass was plentiful and some small homesteaders had their primitive homes. One of the strong horses was Big Feller, which Kurt rode with ease. The two smaller animals carred smaller burdens, expert horsewomen in the shapes of Rose and Charity.

As ever, even on rough trails, they looked totally feminine, clad as they were in Levi jeans, checked shirts and fawn hats – and with their guns around womanly hips they weren't the usual kind of trail rider.

'Hope we're on the right trail,' called out Charity, her blonde hair wisping out from under her almost-new Stetson.

'Fort Worth is about thirty miles due north,' rapped back Kurt Kallon.

'And this disgusting gambling place – Casino Tent?' Rose shouted back. 'Not so far away, I take it – but where are those three rotten killers? They could be anywhere.'

41

'We just have to search for 'em.' Kurt leaned forward, patted the mane of Big Feller. 'We'll find them.'

The day was wearing steadily on towards noon and the heat was building up. During the ride the horses had been raced, then allowed to plod, and at other times to move at a canter. Horses and riders needed water. Kurt knew this and figured to stop when they found any kind of spring.

It was there, with some stunted trees and thorn proving the land held moisture. Kurt swung long legs down to the grassy earth.

'Let's take it easy.'

'Sure. My bum is a bit sore,' said Rose calmly.

He grinned. 'A lady don't talk about her bum – but you're no lady and proud of that fact.'

'How are you gonna kill those three ruffians when we get up to 'em?' asked Charity.

'How should I know? I reckon my gun will do it. Don't think about that. Think about the two *hombres* who've tailed us since we left Cragside.'

'What! Two men! Why didn't yuh tell us?' Rose and Charity swung their feet to the ground. They twisted around and looked back, scanning the undulating landscape behind them. 'Who are they, Kurt?'

He wiped dust from his mouth. 'Who else but that pesky sheriff and his sidekick. Did you think they'd forgotten about the gold I'm carrying?'

'Hmmm.' Rose looked down at the ground. 'It figures, I guess.'

'Have you actually spotted 'em?' Charity shaded her eyes and peered through the strong sunlight.

'Couple of times. They were not so fast at taking cover.' Kurt took a pan from his saddle-bag. 'The hell with them. I'm getting some water from this spring. Looks good enough to slacken a man's thirst.'

'And a lady's!' snapped Rose. She ran fingers through her red hair. 'Damn 'em! I guess they want us dead.'

'And their dirty hands on that gold,' supplied Charity.

Kurt nodded, filled the pan with water and drank from it. He refilled the receptacle and handed it to Rose.

'Don't ladies come first?' snapped the girl. 'Jeeze – what am I doing here with you two? I should have a man of my own.'

'Will they attack us – that damned sheriff an' his pal, I mean?' Rose patted her gun. 'Maybe we should salivate them now.'

'Forget them for the time being. I've got the gold in my saddle-bag. They've got to get me before that gold changes hands. Mind you I'll be glad to hand it over to the law in Fort Worth – when we hit that town.' And Kurt Kallon meant what he said. The gold rankled. The precious yellow stuff wasn't his. Some lone prospector had been killed to get it. Some unknown, an innocent man, had been rubbed out. Kurt didn't like that. He got the strange feeling that the gold he carried in his saddle-bag was a man's soul and life.

Kurt Kallon little realized that two more men were plodding slowly along the same trail, way behind the rogue sheriff and his deputy; two old ruffians who figured the gold was theirs and with stubborn bugs in their minds they thought they could lay hands on it again.

Dad Bowker and the fat man, Snap, had watched the others leave town, watched every move, saw Kurt and his partners move off and had waited until they

saw the sheriff and his sidekick follow. Snap and Dad
Bowker had jumped to the right conclusions, their
cunning old minds being experienced in every trick
and shady play possible in the frontier towns. But they
were a long way behind, with animals that couldn't
break into a canter.

Charity had been thinking. 'Damn the gold – an'
those two rogue lawmen! We're after the brutes who
shot Billy!'

'I haven't forgotten that,' said Kurt slowly. 'I've made
my promises to you two gals. We'll git them skunks.'

Pain and grim determination settled like a mask on
Rose's lovely face. 'I want to fire slugs into at least one
of them dirty *hombres*. Billy was a great brother.'

Kurt nodded and kept busy. They had to eat. He had
to check the horses and see they were watered. Every
five minutes his eyes swept the distant scene beyond
the rocks and hollows for sign of Carl Rigg and his
segundo. But they were lying low somewhere.

'Might try to hit us at night,' muttered Kurt to
himself.

When night did fall they were only a mile from the
grassy hollow in which lay the canvas settlement of
Casino Tent with its mixed bunch of rogues who had
made camp there. Kurt and the girls could see the
lights, yellow kerosene flares. Some of the lights
moved. They were men carrying lanterns in the night
air, men doing chores.

'You think those murderers are here?' muttered
Rose.

'Could be. I'm not sure. Aw, maybe they've gone on to
Fort Worth – but we do know they are gamblers by
nature from the yarns we were told when Billy was
killed.'

Kurt Kallon watched the night scene and the lights but it was too dark to use his spy-glass. He began to realize that he and the girls were in a kind of triangle situation, if the three killers were out there and the tricky sheriff and his partner were also somewhere in the night.

Dad Bowker and Snap had eased their mounts up slowly even though the night air hampered them. By sheer luck they spotted the small fire Kurt and the girls had made on the grassy slope near the spring.

'See 'em', muttered Dad Bowker. 'That's them – that blamed lanky galoot an' the two gals.'

'Sure – gals – no doubt – them in blasted pants like men! Hell, what I'd like to do to them young bitches!' Snap slurred his lecherous comments down his tongue as if he could taste his own evil intent.

'Yeah, bitches in pants,' Dad Bowker added: 'But what the hell – a fat galoot like yuh couldn't git near a young bitch like them!'

'Yeah? Wal, what the hell about you? You're too goddamn old to serve a girl.'

'I ain't so old.' Dad Bowker glared at his partner. He hated the fat man – had hated him even when they'd killed the old prospector and taken his gold. Snap was a fat shit! But maybe he could be used.

'Yeah – wal – lissen, how do we git the gold again? That bastard is fast with guns. An' them bitches – ain't they totin' hardware?'

'Yeah – I saw that on the trail.' Dad Bowker sneered. 'Shee-ite! Whadya know! Gals in pants, be damned – an' toting guns! What next?'

'Should be with child,' leered the other old villain. 'But what the hell! How kin we git hands on that gold, huh?'

'Rush that lanky bastard when he's asleep?' suggested Dad Bowker.

'Mighty dangerous. He's fast – an' maybe he sleeps light.' Snap eased his fat belly and cast a crafty glance at his pal. 'Maybe you could creep up on him. You know – knife him in his sleep! You're not so big as me, podner.'

'You're a fat slob an' I ain't so young as that jasper.'

'You won't do it?'

'The hell with yuh!' snapped the other.

While the two old reprobates were yapping on about ways and means of filching the gold back, there were others on the scene. The crooked sheriff and his deputy had discovered the camp location chosen by Kurt and his partners, mainly because a camp-fire, no matter how small, showed up for miles in the empty land, the only other lights coming from the men in Casino Tent.

'We've got to kill that long bastard,' snarled Carl Rigg, his temper wearing thin at the delays and the long ride.

'Kin we light a fire?' gritted the tall thin deputy. 'I feel a chill in the air.'

'Why the hell didn't yuh pack a wool jacket?' Carl Rigg wished he was on his own with the gold in sight. Gold shared between two wasn't as attractive as a poke of gold just for one.

'Guess I didn't think about it.' The deputy, whose name was Mick Smith, always played second fiddle to his boss. Carl Rigg had chosen the man as deputy, rough-riding the choice to the council in Cragside. He had always figured Mick Smith would be obedient and cover up for him. The tall thin man was pliable but a bit undecisive, and in this way he had been useful in the past – but now Carl Rigg was beginning to wonder about him.

'If we light some damned tinder it might easily be seen by that tall bastard with the gold.'

'Ain't so warm out here,' grumbled the deputy. Then on a new tack: 'Iffen we beat that big *hombre* are we goin' back to Cragside?'

'Why the hell shouldn't we? It's a job with wages—'

'But with that gold – we – we – could jest ride on . . . .' mumbled Mick Smith.

Carl Rigg leered. He was thinking: yeah, I could ride on alone! But just as easy I could mosey back to the sheriff's office in Cragside and spin some yarn as how you'd caught it! Aloud, he said: 'Let's see how this play goes. We've got to beat that big galoot – an' those two gals.'

'They's just women—'

'Yeah? Ain't you seen the hardware they got hung around them damned jean-clad hips?'

'Just females,' grumbled Mick Smith.

'With guns. How many of the housewives in Cragside wear guns like them two?'

'Some of the homesteaders got shotguns—'

'Aw, the hell, Mick Smith – I'm tellin' yuh them two are different.'

Having been verbally bullied into silence the deputy sat and almost sulked, the cold of the night creeping through his shirt. Then, angrily, almost snarling his replies, he asked: 'What in hell are we gonna do? Sit here all night? You said we'd git that gold.'

Carl Rigg nodded. 'Don't forget we're the law back in Cragside. Any tale we tell will be accepted. Iffen we tote a body back we can say anythin'. An' it might come to that.'

'Three bodies – iffen you include them wimmen.'

'Waste of good female flesh,' leered the other man.

'Aw, the hell with it – let's figure somethin' out.'

Mick Smith was silent again, thinking no matter what Carl Rigg plotted, the tall lanky *hombre* had to be salivated.

Way off in the cold night air, with the stars glinting in the heavens as a ceiling to the mere human beings, Kurt Kallon put some more brushwood on to his fire and watched the sparks vainly try to reach out to the sky. It was time to rest, get some sleep. He knew he wouldn't enjoy much of that with enemies in the night but the girls had to rest. The horses were still, ground-hitched, bellies full of grass. He would rub the animals down in the morning.

He couldn't be sure, but he had this hunch that the three killers they chased were down in the gambling tent-town. They'd prefer that location to Fort Worth because the law was strong in that town. Fort Worth's town marshal, Jake Duerr, was a strong character who liked to know every newcomer to that growing, bustling town. That was quite a chore, but he did it. Kurt had heard about him.

He sat close to the fire. He figured he'd much prefer to lie close to Rose or Charity but that wasn't a choice at the moment with menacing men in the night. He sat still, a big man who could be very quiet when he chose, a quality that had saved his skin more than once in the past on dubious trails.

And so he heard the little sounds, almost whispers in the cold night air; except that these noises were created by human feet trying to approach closely and silently. Kurt sat quite still. His hand inched slowly to his Peacemaker, very slowly. Now who the hell was creeping up? They weren't too good at imitating the Indian. In fact they were creating a number of small identifiable sounds like loosening stones from the soil and cracking twigs. He even knew they were on hands and knees. He heard one mutter and an almost inaudible curse as a thorn stuck into flesh. But the human speech in the night was a bit of a puzzler. He'd been expecting the crooked sheriff Carl Rigg and his deputy but these few words were in a different voice.

Now where had he heard this gruff old husky talk?

Kurt glanced at the motionless figures of the two girls, huddled in blankets, like sacks, except that they weren't two sacks but two lovely feminine creatures who had tempted him and taken him in the way of man and woman in human life. He didn't regret making love to two young girls. He figured he loved them both, but was that possible? The bible-punchers in the town mission halls preached one man to one woman – but Kurt Kallon knew that rough life wasn't all that perfect.

The encrouching sounds came nearer. He put fingers to his gun, felt the smooth butt, knew the power of death lay in that weapon. He kept really still, all his senses concentrated on the sounds, as if he could visualize what was happening even without sighting. So Carl Rigg figured to take the gold! Yeah, the lure of the yellow metal had tempted better men than the sheriff.

But all at once other sounds in the night reached Kurt's ears and added to the puzzles. Swiftly, he knew some other men were approaching his camp-fire. Two men – on their feet – not two crawling menaces but men walking upright, carefully but nevertheless decisively.

Now what the hell was it all about? He knew it was time for a man to make a play. Kurt reached for his Peacemaker, glad of the fast-draw holster, and at the same time he whipped around, rising like a giant to his feet, the camp-fire and the girls behind him.

The first things he saw just within range of the fire's glow were the two crawling figures of Dad Bowker and his crafty pal, Snap. It was a surprise seeing them, so far from Cragside. So they'd trailed him.

And then, beyond, standing upright, were two taller figures in the menacing shapes of Carl Rigg and his deputy. Hell! Two damned parties were after the gold – and prepared to kill to get it.

The next few moments were a confusing jumble of movements and gun-shots, barking Colts crazily sending out their death messages.

Kurt added his thunderous gun-shots. He saw his target dive to the ground with lightning speed, as if sensing the Peacemaker in the night air. The swiftness of the man's dive did not suggest he'd been hit by a bullet. Kurt muttered an old frontier curse and blasted off another shot at a shadowy figure but there was nothing definite about these speeding slugs. Answering bullets came his way and he had to duck. He thought one of the crawling old men had shot at him but in the confusion and the darkness – broken only by the flashes of gun-flame – he wasn't sure.

Then some more deadly cracking shots cut the night and there were simultaneous screams, men screeching their agony. Kurt crouched, knees bent, his eyes peering through the darkness. He was ready to blast off a shot at anything that moved. But nothing did walk or stand in the gloom, nothing that he could see.

But the smell of burnt gunpowder hung in the still night air and somewhere a man moaned in what Kurt sensed were death sounds. Who was out there and dying? Had he hit the sheriff or his deputy? He didn't think so. The figure he had targeted had dived and escaped a slug in the gut by a split second.

Of course, the two girls were on their feet and by his side with their hardware at the ready, although they had not fired a shot. He glanced interestedly at Rose. She was topless, wearing only some white cotton drawers, apparently her night wear. A semi-naked lady with a huge Colt .45!

Charity was equally scantily clad. Being feminine, they were panting their questions.

'Who's out there, Kurt? What's going on?'

'Men with guns,' he rapped. 'Just watch it! You're both targets.'

Their tied-up horses some yards away, hitched to the stunted trees, were moving restlessly, frightened by the gunfire. But ropes held them secure.

'Carl Rigg and his deputy, no less. We knew they were around. Seems they really want that gold.'

'Seems a lot of shot cut the night air.'

'I fired,' said Kurt. 'But I figure I missed by a hair's-breath. I think I'll go see what's out there in the night.'

Suddenly, two pairs of naked arms clutched at him and held him back. 'Watch out, Kurt! You're our man. Where would we be if you ended up dead?'

'I'm alive,' he chuckled. 'But I want to take a look. You see, the pesky sheriff and his pard were not the only men out in this night air.'

'Others?'

'Yeah – them two old villains, Snap and Dad Bowker.'

'No! Are yuh sure?'

'I saw 'em. An' some galoot stopped a slug and screamed his death song.'

'Who?'

'That's what I aim to find out. Just stick around, gals – an' don't fire at me. I think they've taken off, anyway.'

He stepped forward beyond the dull glow of their camp-fire. He tuned his eyes to the darkness, inching, step by step. He was soon beyond the perimeter of their camp, the grassy slope leading down to the valley floor. A mile away lay Casino Tent, still full of activity, judging by the sounds that carried through the night air. Men were there, drinking and gambling, among them quite probably the murderers of Billy Graham.

Kurt Kallon could not forget his promise to the girls. He'd said in words of absolute finality that he'd help track down the three killers. He'd made it a promise. He repeated the words full of significance many times. There was no way he'd retract. The very basis of his relationship with Rose and Charity lay in that grim solemn promise.

Kurt soon stumbled over two dead bodies out there in the night, the fatso Snap and his older partner, Dad Bowker, sprawled near some thorn bush as if they'd dived for cover in the ratapan of bullets but had failed to find refuge. So Carl Rigg and his sidekick had gunned down the two oldsters! Kurt knew he hadn't shot at them.

Blood formed gruesome pools as the two men lay flat on their backs, hands outstretched and eyes now sightless and fixed. The oldsters had died as they had lived, lawless old galoots with greed on their minds. Kurt looked for a gun but could not find one. Probably a Colt lay somewhere on the dark land. And somewhere among the big rocks the old-timers had hidden mounts.

Time to look for the critters when daylight flowed over the land again.

Kurt holstered his gun. The two old idiots had been slaughtered by Carl Rigg and his partner in death and crime. It was a sure thing those two were holed up in the night some way off.

Kurt turned around and went slowly back to the glow of his distant camp-fire against which he could see the outlines of the two girls.

He told them what he had found. 'Death and gold,' he muttered. 'They always go together.'

'The two old men!' exclaimed Rose, red hair flowing.

'Old fools – or old villains,' muttered Kurt. He began to smile again when he glanced at Rose's full semi-naked shape. All right, he had seen her attributes many times, in close intimacy, but she always looked good. Come to think of it, so did Charity. Yeah, he was a lucky *hombre*!

The sound of barking guns piercing the night air was something that carried a long way in the silent night, as any range rider knew. As Hec Redman bent over Kid Curtis he heard the distant shots of the Colt clearly and strangely as if they were much closer than a mile and a half away. Hec Redman, a man of instincts when out in the wilds, scowled and wondered crazily who was out there and who was shooting.

Harry, the 'breed, had the same instinct for detecting grief; he had strange hunches. Both men stared around in the darkness, seeing nothing of any definable shape, but only the empty space of the night and the endless land.

'What the hell's goin' on 'way back?' Hec Redman ground out.

'Ain't from the Tent.'

'Rannigans out there.'

'Using guns on each other. That weren't no drunken lot.'

'Nope. Wal, could be any galoots . . . .'

'Yeah – could be – but . . . .'

'You figure some feller is out there – after us?' mocked Hec Redman.

'I dunno. I always figger there's some gink after us . . . .'

'That's horse shit! We're miles from anywhere. Now how the hell do you figger that? Gimme a hand with the Kid. He's out.'

'Maybe he should stay out. Guess he's got his *dinero* in his pockets, huh?'

'Yeah. But he ain't dead. He's lost a lot of blood from his shoulder wound. Are yuh gonna git him back on his hoss or let him die out here?'

Harry was still listening intently, ears and senses trying to tune to sounds too distant for even his acute Indian ancestry to solve.

'We git him back, I guess. Damn him! He's spoilt the night. Hell, let's git on wi' it! Jeeze, we should ha' been making money this night an' not baby-minding! Young bastard!'

FIVE

Rose Merit sat with her knees hunched up near the camp-fire comforted a little by the glow from the darkness and the dangers beyond. There was some consolation. Kurt was lying in a quiet huddle and she knew he'd leap up instantly the second any danger threatened. He was that kind of man. He was also a nice *hombre*, a man any girl would be proud to call her own. She could hardly do that. She knew Charity loved him, made claims on him, the blonde bitch, her special friend.

Of course, she loved Charity, as she had liked Billy, her other trail pal. Poor Billy – dead – killed violently by ruthless gunnies. She could hardly bear to think about it.

She moved restlessly, huddled in a blanket, a little bit scared. Oh, she and Charity always put on the act that they were terribly modern, a bit contemptuous of the crinoline age, but in truth they were mere women in a violent frontier landscape. Even the comparative civilization of a big cow-town held dangers for women on their own. That was why she and Charity wore guns.

Kurt had told her: 'We'll visit Casino Tent in daylight. We've run out of time thisaday. Anyway, it's

the last place on earth for two gals to walk into at
night – too many rogues and killers, I guess. The sight
of you two might start a riot.'

'I have a long taffeta dress in my saddle-bags,' Rose
told him.

'Ain't seen yuh wear it . . . .'

'I keep it for best wear,' she said sweetly. 'I might
even get an invitation to a dance or a party some day.'

'Not on the trails we're taking, Rose, me darlin'!'

Kurt was sweet. But was Kurt Kallon the man to
share the rest of her life, raise a family? A woman
should have children – a man, too! Well, she had a
man, in a sense, but crazily she was sharing him with
her damned new pal. Of course, some wonderful jasper
might suddenly appear in Charity's life and take her
away and raise a brood but, hell, that might be
anywhere in this vast land. If Charity got a man, she
might not see her again! Oh, tarnation! Life was
complicated!

As Rose tried to sleep despite her rambling
thoughts, Kurt Kallon was doing almost the same, and
contriving to keep ears and other senses alert for a new
resurgence of danger, his fingers near his gun butt.
Had the crooked sheriff and his pal taken off to some
point a long way down the trail? Seemed that way. The
night air was so still that even the movement of a
skunk's tail a mile away might be heard! Carl Rigg was
somewhere in the night but the location might be miles
away.

Casino Tent had its share of hardcases. Were Billy's
three killers down there at the bottom of that grassy
slope? Well, night-time was the worst moment to visit
the tent – especially with two young and attractive
females to protect.

Kurt's thoughts rambled on, bemused by half-sleep. Maybe it would be safer for him to visit Casino Tent alone. Maybe that way, as a lone man among other armed strangers, he'd stand a chance of making discoveries, finding out if the three savage killers were in the area. Maybe they'd gone on to Fort Worth. He didn't think so. They would not pass up a chance to indulge in more gambling, being the type of reckless gamblers they were.

Of course, he could mosey around at any time. That meant leaving Rose and Charity to fend for themselves. Well, hell, they packed hoglegs! And they could send a tin can spinning with the best of shooting men! Yeah, maybe a daylight stroll around Casino Tent might pay off.

Strangely, while Kurt was full of his own half-formed thoughts and Rose had a head full of rambling ideas, Charity Brendan was not entirely asleep but also troubled by thoughts.

She was a bit jealous of Rose! Maybe Kurt liked red hair better than blonde. She realized that must be a trivial thought because Rose and herself were persons and not just dolls with varied coloured hair, shaped in different ways. And if Kurt Kallon could not see them as real women – then to heck with Kurt Kallon. He surely was not the only galoot in this wide world! Cragside had its share of young personable horny men!

Still, she loved Kurt. At least she figured she loved him. Oh, damn him! He was too big, too virile, too masculine! But of course lovely with it. Trouble was Rose felt the same way about him! Damn her! Rose was a wonderful friend, and when Billy was alive they'd been a great trio. But Rose wanted Kurt! It was a scandalous state of affairs for two women . . . to share the same man. All the other womenfolk of Cragside had their men, legal and proper, with a roof over their heads and children to substantiate the marriage.

It was crazy for two gals to love the same ornery galoot and even want him in bed. What the hell would the other females of Cragside – or any other town – make of that terrible set-up?

Night and sheer fatigue contributed to sound sleep. The girls lost their confused thoughts and slid into the comforting pit of deep sleep and even Kurt Kallon, knowing the need to sense danger if it arose, went into the embrace of total sleep. Only the occasional move-ment of the horses ground-hitched among the twisted, stunted trees brought any sound into the night air.

Then Kurt sat up – bolt upright. Confusion and daylight hit him. He'd been dead out. Alertness and sanity swept into his brain. Was something wrong?

No! It was just a new day, damned early but the sun was above the horizon. A new day and new problems – or maybe they were just the old problems in a new light. Yeah, killers to find. Two girls to protect. Horses to rub down and water. Hell, he had to get going! He knew clearly what he had to do.

Sure. He had to ride down into Casino Tent, alone, with daylight around him, his Peacemaker full of slugs. The girls would have to be safely encamped in a secure place. Anyway, it shouldn't take long for him to ascertain if the three killers were anywhere close to the gambling tent. He still wasn't sure about that.

'Leaving us!' exclaimed Rose.

'Won't be for damned long . . . .'

'Out here – alone . . . .' Charity looked dubious. She had been washing at the rock-bound bubbling spring and she was candidly unconcerned about being topless.

She looked one hundred-per-cent lovely female, sturdy, fresh from her wash, eyes gleaming when she saw the sexual interest in Kurt's visage. Of course, the horny bastard would be the same if he was staring at a half-naked Rose!

'We've got to find a better base – then I'll ride down to that damned Casino Tent an' discover once and for all if those miserable killers are established there.'

They packed up the camp and rode off some miles down a rocky defile. Then Kurt found what seemed a good spot for a new camp. There was a cave entrance with plenty of cover in the shape of thorn bush and overhanging mesquite. A nook would do fine for the horses. There wasn't any water but for the moment the water canteens were full. During the ride Kurt had sat tall in the saddle, his black shirt making him seem totally masculine, and he had been watchful for any sign of other riders for miles around. Carl Rigg and his twisty deputy would still have the odour of gold in their nostrils, metaphorically speaking. They were somewhere. Damn them! They should be dead like the unfortunate Dad Bowker and Snap they had gunned down.

He waved a temporary farewell to the girls and rode down the defile, gun loaded, his rifle snug in the saddle holster.

Big Feller moved easily, strong haunches carrying Kurt over the rough land, picking a way through rocks and going smoothly when the land became level and grassy. The sun was climbing, with warmth in the air. All the same, he figured autumn would arrive in a few weeks and the days would get cold.

The tent settlement looked oddly peaceful, with the big canvas showing little sign of the hectic gambling activities of the night. Smaller tents were established on various flat locations in the terrain; apparently these were living-quarters for the hangers-on of the gambling joint.

Kurt Kallon rode easily and carefully near to the big canvas and hitched Big Feller to a convenient post. He walked into the big tent.

A tall thin man in a pink shirt watched him with strange interest, noting he was a new face. Among many other weird characteristics, this man, one Slim Beeny, with fair womanish hair, made it his business to scrutinize any newcomer to the scene. A new man, a new face, could be a person more to his liking than the roughnecks who came to Casino Tent. Slim Beeny followed Kurt into the tent. The man moved with effeminate grace, a hand on his jean-clad hip.

As Kurt stared around, noting that there were already a few gentry flicking through decks of cards at some tables, Slim Beeny came up close to Kurt, too close, the tall range-rider thought. He took an instant dislike to the fellow's proximity, although he noted the galoot did not pack a gun or a gun-belt. His fancy jeans, spotless in a world where dirt and horse-muck were part of living, were hitched close on a slim waist.

Slim Beeny spoke gently, almost prissily.

'Care to buy me a drink, feller?'

Kurt grinned. 'Yeah. Why not? I want to talk to some gink.'

'Oh, dear, darlin' man, get me a whiskey!'

Kurt obliged at the plank bar.

'You seen many newcomers to this place? Like three hardcases who figure to gamble hard?'

'I see them all!' Slim Beeny gestured like a woman. 'Gamblers? Well, they are all gamblers here, man.'

'These three I guess might not be much different to the rest of the bunch who get in a place like this, but I was told one was a 'breed, one a young feller – little more than a youth – and the other an older jasper.'

'Names?' Slim Beeny smiled sweetly and Kurt felt fresh distaste for him.

'I got no names . . . .'

'Why do you want 'em?'

'I'd like to kill 'em.'

The other man shuddered. 'Dear man, why do you want to kill things? I think I'll move away from this place – too crude by far! Men! Oh, dear! Yes, I think I did see three *hombres* of the kind you mention.'

'Yeah? Seems it's lucky I got talkin' to you, huh?'

Slim Beeny swept him a coy glance. 'I wonder if you're lucky for me? I mean – oh, never mind – I can see you're not my type.'

'The three galoots, Feller? Are they around? Sleepin' it off in a tent somewhere, huh?'

'Dearie me – no. 'Breed, you say – thin face? Young galoot – nice boy, I figured. And another hard cuss who I wouldn't like to hold my hand? Yeah – that was them.'

'That could be them,' said Kurt impatiently, looking curiously at this man. 'Answers the description I got, an' three of them being together can't be coincidence.'

'They killed two men,' said Slim Beeny in awe. 'Two nice men, I hear. Not my type – but never mind – killed 'em.'

'What happened?'

'Money, I guess – what else? One got shot up a bit, tho.'

'Shot up?'

'Yeah. A shoulder wound I think. I dunno every-thing, dear man. I was a long way off.' Slim Beeny shuddered. 'Just as well. I don't like guns, you know. My Mom said guns were evil an' people should love each other – and I agree. We should be more loving.'

'Well, we ain't,' said Kurt steadily. 'Although the day may arrive when we'll outlaw death by hardware. What happened to these three ginks?'

'Oh!' Slim waved his hands around. 'They just rode off into the night, I hear. The young lad was bleeding badly, I believe. Pity. Seemed a nice boy.'

Kurt nodded. His eyes swept the sparsely-filled tent and he got the hunch that his three murderers were not in sight. With a curious glance at the man in the pink shirt and the wavy blond hair, he returned to his hitched horse. He returned the look of hard scrutiny given him by a man at the tent entrance, whose fingers were hitched in a thick gun-belt. The man wore coarse stovepipe tweeds smeared with stains. His beard was a grey-and-ginger mixture. Kurt got the feeling he was paid to watch entrants to the Casino Tent. Kurt grinned mockingly and grabbed the leathers of Big Feller.

So one of the three men had stopped a slug and was bleeding badly! Kurt felt grim. He thought he had located the three killers. The sparse descriptions matched the earlier descriptions given in the saloon when Billy had been killed. Yeah all his hunches said these were the murderers.

So they had rode out. And the young gunny was bleeding. That should hamper their flight.

He was on to a lead. Now which way had the rotten bastards gone? North, south, east or west. Could be the trail to Fort Worth because the rest of the terrain was badland, fit only for scrub cattle; there were few settlements in sight.

He rode slowly up the long incline. He figured on taking an easy trail along to the cave and the girls.

If Kurt Kallon had had spy-glass vision, he'd have hurtled Big Feller into full lope. His intuitions had limitations. He did not, for instance, visualize the scene around the cave where the girls and the horses were stationed.

Rose and Charity had been taken by surprise. They'd been trying to get rid of trail dirt and sweat in the small trickle of spring water which they had discovered a good hundred yards past the cave. Kurt had told them to stick to the cave, where they could hide and where even the horses were in cover. But the pool of water was such a tempting lure for two girls who liked cleanliness above all.

True, the horses were hidden, but when they discovered the pool they could not resist the desire to wash thoroughly and get rid of horse odour and trail sweat.

Rose rolled up her baggy work-type jeans and waded into the clear pool, squealing her delight when the cool water swished nearly up to her knees.

'Come on in, Charity!'

'Looks lovely!' the blonde girl agreed. 'But, hey, didn't Kurt tell us to stick to the cave?'

'Oh, pooh! Kurt's too wary. Anyway, who's around here? Ain't even a rattler for miles.'

'We were told—'

'Come on in. Won't take much time. Kurt will be back soon, I guess. Then he'll be issuing orders again, I suppose.'

Charity smiled and giggled. Swiftly, she rolled the work-pants up to her knees. 'We should take a real bath – nothing on.'

'Maybe you're right. Should we?'

'Why not? Might be a long time before we get the chance to sluice away in a pool like this. Don't know why Kurt didn't notice it in the first place. The animals should have given signals that there was water around.'

Being young and full of zest for life, they did not waste any more time on useless talk but swiftly got out of their clothes and waded into the pool. They splashed around and gave ringing cries of delight when the cool spring soothed warm naked skin.

They were naked in a wide empty land – or so they figured. The blue sky, patched by a few fleeting clouds, was their roof and the soft air, warmed by the early sun, sufficient clothing.

They did not know that two grim men had watched them. The two hard jaspers had left horses a long way behind, ground-hitched by heavy boulders, as they searched the terrain.

The men figured Kurt Kallon was somewhere around. He was the man with the poke of gold. And gold held a permanent lure for grim men in a frontier land.

They'd heard the girlish cries of delight from a long way off. Two girls, fooling around, they figured. But where was the man they feared? The *hombre* with the big smoke-pole?

When Carl Rigg and his companion, Mick Smith, pin-pointed the source of the joyous cries, they could hardly believe their luck.

'Them bitches. Naked! Washin' in thet pool, would yuh believe.'

'Where the hell's that gunny?'

The two men crouched behind a convenient boulder,

scoured by centuries of winds and winter rains to a smooth surface, and stared almost in disbelief.

'Goddamn naked bitches! Wal, we got 'em to rights!'

'Where's that tall devil? Cain't be far off!'

'Yeah. We'll wait. If he's around, we'll git the drop on him, sure thing. Remember he's got the gold. It's the gold we want – not the sight of naked wimmen.'

'Yeah. Gold kin buy a helluva lot of bitches with their drawers down!' And Mick Smith indulged in some stupid laughter.

His third-rate amusement wasn't heard by Charity and Rose as they continued to splash the cool water over their bodies. Carl Rigg did entertain some lewd thoughts at the sight of the girls – and then he knew he held a full deck of cards.

'We'll git them gals!' he jerked at his one-time deputy. 'We can use 'em. Hostages – for gold!'

'Hostages, huh! Now why didn't I think of that!'

''Cos you ain't got the brains,' sneered the bent sheriff.

'Now look here, Mr Rigg. Don't try to rile me. You need me. We've worked together for a long time. An' maybe you cain't handle that lanky *hombre* an' the two gals an' git that gold all at once.'

'Who says,' Carl Rigg sneered again. He stared hard at his deputy and saw a useless man, someone he could dispose of if a sizeable poke of gold was to hand. But maybe this wasn't the moment to get tough with Mick Smith.

'We've got to grab them bitches,' he said suddenly, switching his thoughts around. He stared above the boulder, nasty grim lines etched into his face, his dusty hat pulled down low.

'Let's go,' lisped the other man.

They were so sure of their advantages that they simply advanced openly, guns in hard fists. They were both thinking: what the hell can two naked bitches do against two galoots with hardware!

And the reasoning was correct. Rose and Charity had left their guns beside their heaped-up clothes.

There was no place to run, no cover, and certainly no Kurt Kallon to hand.

Naturally, they tried to fend off the men who grabbed at them and actually took little notice of the guns, but the two dubious law-men were strong enough to handle two girls, even swift and supple females like Rose and Charity. Rough long arms went out to grab at them. Carl Rigg gripped Charity by an arm and dug his gun into her naked skin.

'Quit struggling or I'll blow a hole in that young body of yourn!'

She took little notice of the grated warning. Suddenly, Carl Rigg hit her with a fist, on the side of her head, and when she sank to the ground in a daze, he stood over her and pointed his gun at her naked body. Charity glanced up appealingly.

'Don't shoot!'

The rogue sheriff knew the girl was worth more alive and well than dead. He grinned, bent over the blonde girl, gun close to her head.

'My – my – but ain't you the lovely!'

Mick Smith gloated at the sight of Rose, her red hair wet and straggling down her neck. His gun, pointing menacingly, served to steady her. She cast wild glances all around and saw that she and Charity were trapped.

'What – what – do you want?' she panted.

'I'd like you in a little while,' leered Mick Smith, 'but that gold would do for right now. Where is it?'

'Kurt took the poke with him,' flashed the girl and then she wondered if that had been a wise remark.

'An' where the hell is he?'

'He'll be back any moment – an' he'll kill you two bastards.'

'Where the blazes are your hosses?' demanded Carl Rigg.

'Not far off.' Rose figured to stall for time, hoping that Kurt would in fact suddenly appear.

Carl Rigg thought that all the cards were stacked in his favour and he grinned nastily. 'Wal, we want that gold – an' that damned lanky feller out of the way, so I reckon we'll just hang around until he turns up, gold an' all, and then we'll plug him stone dead. In the meantime, with two naked bitches on hand maybe it's time for a man to have a bit of fun.'

He reached down and hauled Charity to her feet. Held her close, his rasping hand on her naked back. She struggled vigorously but he held her and seemed to enjoy the antagonsm. He slid his gun into the holster so that he could use two hands to subdue the girl. Mick Smith decided that he, too, could copy his pal. He grabbed at Rose and held her tight. She fought back, her naked body struggling against his strength. He, too, had holstered his gun, sure that the girl was no threat. He could handle her. By thunder, he'd do more than merely restrain her. Gold was lovely stuff but so was a naked girl.

Mick Smith wrestled with the girl and his rough hands were all over her body, struggle as she might. He thought crazily that he'd kiss this supple lovely bitch and his rough mouth sought her lips, his beard rasping against her skin. She felt a loathing of this hateful man and she screamed loudly. How she wished she had her gun! She'd have killed this brute without compunction.

Carl Rigg seemed to be enjoying his struggle with Charity, his hands grabbing at her while she fought him off. So they wanted Kurt dead and their hands on the gold!

Grunting and gasping, Carl Rigg found that Charity was more than a handful of naked womanly flesh because she kicked at him, knowing the rough tactics the saloon girls sometimes used against men. She made him yell in sudden pain. She kicked again, low in his body. He snarled at her, stopped laughing at her struggles and her resistance to him. He swung a blow at her face and connected. She moaned slightly and felt blood trickle down her lips. She thrust at the man, her heart beating with fear while sweat suddenly appeared on her body. She realized she was going to lose this fight. What then? Would he kill her or – what would he do?

Rose was on the ground again, huddled, her breathing hard and gasping, and Mick Smith was standing over the defenceless girl, gloating, sure that he could do anything to her now.

Suddenly, a man on a big horse tore with pounding hooves right up to the ground near the pool and hurled himself at Mick Smith as he stood over Rose, his fingers ready to unbuckle his trouser belt.

Kurt rammed into the man and sent him flying. The deputy thudded to hard earth. He stared at Kurt's savage face and then tried to haul his Colt from the holster. Lying flat on his back, it wasn't an easy trick to perform. He got the gun clear, sure thing, and his finger was on the trigger, with intent to kill, when Kurt fired his own guns swiftly. He was too fast for the deputy. Kurt's Peacemaker exploded and sent a slug tearing into Mick Smith's exposed chest. A nasty hole was torn in the flesh and muscle and blood spurted like a horrible jet. The man twitched once and then died with a twist to his mouth that made his visage look like a grisly mask.

Carl Rigg saw it all in split seconds. With Kurt's gun on the dead man, he had a moment's advantage. He dived away like a crazy animal, boots digging at loose earth and grass. Charity screamed at Kurt.

'Kill him! Kill him!'

Kurt whipped his weapon around with speed and at that second the sheriff dived to the earth as if instinct crashed a warning into his brain that he was in danger.

Kurt's slug hit rock. He fired again but Carl Rigg was tearing across the ground like some escaping creature on all fours. Kurt tried to get a bead on the man once more, intent on killing him, but Big Feller jigged in fright at the gunshots and got in the way. Carl Rigg flung into a rocky crevice, ignoring prickly thorn bush, and then scuttled with wild speed for his very life.

He forgot about trying a wild shot in self-defence against this grim man with the Peacemaker. He was fleeing desperately.

Kurt ran after the rogue sheriff and in his haste he fell over a jagged rock in his path. He sprawled, got almost instantly to his feet again only to find his target had disappeared.

And then Charity screamed. 'Hold me, Kurt! I'm scared!'

Rose howled some girlish fear. The voices stopped Kurt in his tracks and he swung uncertainly around. Carl Rigg scuttled like a creature in fright. Luck was with him. He got away, down the broken terrain, bent double, running a weaving path between rocks and boulders.

Kurt found himself being detained by two girls who hung on to him in fright. He tightened his lips as he realized this was the first time he'd seen Rose and Charity so scared. Then he swung angrily.

'Why in hell are you two stark naked?'

'We were bathing . . . .'

'You left the cave where I'd told yuh to hide!'

'We wanted to splash in the water.'

'Yeah – goddamn it – why cain't yuh do as you are told?'

'Why the devil should we? You don't own us!' Rose was the first to recover her old confidence.

'If I did I'd feel like giving you two a hiding,' he flared. 'You could be dead by now – an' worse!'

'But Kurt, darling, you came to the rescue like Sir Galahad!' mocked Charity. 'You're our man – and that's what you are for.'

He glared and then slowly grinned. 'Aw, hell – at least I got one of 'em!'

Kurt strode over to the dead deputy, sprawling in his own blood among the rocky debris and tufts of grass. Kurt stared, deep lines drawn on his face.

'Dead as all hell. An' I killed him.'

'Good!' snapped Rose. 'He was all set to molest us – an' plug you when you rode up.'

'Iffen he could have taken me by surprise.'

'They might have done just that.'

Kurt slapped Rose on the buttocks. 'Git some damned clothes on!' he roared. 'An' you, too, Charity. Gawd, I ain't never seen anythin' like it!'

'Ain't you?' Charity cheeked. 'You ain't never seen another naked lady? You liar!'

'They were after the gold,' he snapped. 'And Carl Rigg has gotten clean away.'

As if to prove the comment, they suddenly heard the drumming of hooves from way off, a man on a tearing horse. Carl Rigg had hit the saddle and was making his escape.

'I had the chance to kill him,' gritted Kurt Kallon. 'An' you two gals got in my way.'

Rose was slipping into her gear, looking shapely and provocative in jean pants only.

'With the smell of gold in his dirty nose, he'll be back somewheres on this trail.'

'Yeah.' Kurt plucked the deputy badge from the dead man. 'You could be right. But don't forget we want those three killers dead. Let's talk about them – then ride after them.'

SIX

They had to hole up because Kid Curtis was bleeding again, looking distinctly faint and barely able to sit his horse. They had travelled for part of the night and by pure chance had come across this old adobe-and-reed shack at the jagged entrance to a small defile. They were a few miles distant from Casino Tent, in the wilds as far as any other inhabitants were concerned. The old semi-ruined shack seemed a good enough place to rest awhile. Hec Redman made the decision, taking the lead as usual. Angry, in a dirty temper, he swung down from his mount and then hauled Kid Curtis to the ground, so roughly that the young fellow fell from his saddle like a sack of spuds and hit the earth forcefully. He lay in a huddle and groaned.

'Aw, shit! Maybe he should ha' died!'

'What do you figure to do about him?'

'Patch him up, I guess. I got an old shirt in my saddle-bag that will tear into strips an' make bandages and a sling.'

Harry, the 'breed, pulled the leather thong of his hat down into his mouth and chewed on it.

'He's got his money – in a pocket – I notice . . . .'

'Yeah. He stashed that OK afore fallin' from that

73

durned hoss of his. Aw, blast – let's see what it's like in this old shack, huh?'

'Place to shack up,' commented Harry. 'Then what?'

'It's a big country,' sneered the other man. 'Maybe we kin rob somebody afore we hit Fort Worth.'

'Should we trail into that town? I've head a jasper called Jake Duerr is a pretty hot-stuff town marshal right there.'

'Well, the hell with the law! Let's just hole up. You're yappin' a lot, Harry! Ain't like yuh!' And with that snapped answer, Hec Redman hauled the wounded young man into the dark hole of the adobe shack. He paused and peered around, sniffing the air grimly. 'Stinks!'

'Yeah. Black as all hell, also.' Harry peered into the corners of the old Indian shack. 'Some loner lived hyar – long time past.'

'You're the 'breed. You sense these things.' Hec Redman leaned over Kid Curtis and heard the moaning stop and some wild words issue.

'You skunks ain't takin' my *dinero*!'

'Seems the Kid ain't so delirious. What the hell!' Hec Redman sneered. 'Aw, let's git him bandaged. Iffen he's gonna ride with us, he'd better be fit for the job.'

While they were busy in the darkness, with no light from a cloud-obscured moon, Harry gave a sudden exclamation.

'Thought I smelled death.'

'What the blazes are you talkin' about now?'

'We got a dead man here!'

'Wha-a-at!' For a killer, Hec Redman was suddenly disgusted as he peered through the gloom and into the corner Harry indicated. Sure as there were coyotes in the night, they could make out the huddled body of a

man who had been dead for some days or maybe a
week. He was white, a youngish man in range clothes
and now smelling to high heaven. Harry turned the
body over with a foot.

'Shot! Some Goddamned wanderer, I guess.'

'Like us!' said Hec Redman savagely. 'Jeeze, maybe
Kid Curtis will join him in death. I don't like this
place.'

'We could put our bedrolls out in the open – on the
grass – near the hosses.'

'Better than bunkin' with a dead man!'

Hec's temper was more than usually savage. Few
things seemed to be going right, he figured. They
should be in comfort, drinking and gambling in the
Casino Tent with others of a like mind. Instead, they
were in a kind of trap with a wounded man on hand,
their food a bit low and no clear idea of where they
wanted to settle.

As Hec Redman tore an old shirt into strips and
bandaged the wound in the young fellow's shoulder, he
wished Kid Curtis would die so that they could ride
out come sun-up, high, wide and handsome with the
freedom to get into any adventure that promised
profit.

They were stuck, and with a dead corpse in the
shack to boot! Hell!

In this bad situation the three men passed the
night, sleeping in the open. With the new day warming
the land and offering the freedom to three hardcases to
ride to hell and back, they lit a fire and boiled water for
their coffee. All they had to eat was dry bread in crusts.
They had figured to eat in style at Casino Tent. If
they'd won some money, by hook or by crook, they'd
maybe have got the chance to do some womanizing.

There were some bitches in petticoats at the gambling tent, they knew.

'Sonofabitch!' snarled Hec Redman and he stared at the sprawling Kid Curtis. A blanket covered the young fellow. 'Is he ready to ride? We can't stay here.'

'We can't go back to Casino Tent.' Harry was his usual morose self. With his black beard, the result of a week's riding and little soap, he looked a grisly unattractive man. Hec Redman was no better, his clothes dirty with sleeping rough.

'We'll head for Fort Worth,' decided Hec. 'Ain't nothin' else! And the sooner we git away from that stinkin' corpse in the shack the better. Dead men give me the creeps!'

Harry couldn't smile. His lips twisted. 'That's good, heh! Heh! You've sure deaded a few in your time!'

'We'll ride out soon.' Hec Redman moved over to Kid Curtis and shook the man roughly. 'Hey! You ready to vamoose, Kid?'

Slowly, with time seemingly of no account in the wide empty spaces around them, the sky above becoming bluer with every passing minute, they spotted a distant black shape down the sloping broken land that could only indicate an approaching rider. Harry and Hec fixed steady wary eyes on the moving black object, silent, tensed, just wondering who was coming this way and why. A rider, slowly taking definite shape in the cool morning air, becoming a person of unknown possibilities, was surely coming towards them.

'He ain't taking the lower ground,' said Hec Redman. 'He sure as hell is coming straight towards us.'

'Headin' for this shack.' Harry sat hunched, waiting, not moving, looking like all his Indian ancestors.

Some minutes later they could make out the details of the stranger, his brown sturdy mare, the checked fleece jacket and the guns. Yes, the guns! A rifle in a saddle holster and a handgun in a holster. Maybe the man was just another wanderer, maybe from Fort Worth, where else? But Hec and Harry, with the instincts of a cunning life on many trails, started to wonder about the travelling man.

'Headin' for this damned shack! Now why?'

'Maybe he just figures to lie low – like us.'

'He ain't welcome – unless he's got *dinero*.'

'Yeah. We kin always use *dinero*,' agreed Harry, and he sat as still as a rock.

And then they were spotted, the three tethered animals giving the warning that others were near the old adobe shack. Still the youngish man did not alter his course but came on slowly and deliberately to the spot where they sat near their fire and the horses.

Then: 'Howdy. You been here awhile?'

'Some time,' agreed Hec Redman.

'Yuh seen a body in that shack?'

Hec Redman exchanged a glance with his partner.

'Yeah. Stinks a bit.'

'Don't talk like that!'

'Why in hell not? All dead cusses stink.' Hec Redman stared, thinning his lips, suspicious. He saw the hard-riding outfit, the guns, the lean wiry frame of this youngish man. 'You knew there was a dead galoot in hyar?'

'Yes. He's my brother.'

Harry's face was almost hidden by his misshapen hat. 'What do yuh want with a dead brother, mister?'

'I figured to bury him good an' proper.' The young man flicked a glance at the blanket covering the huddled shape of Kid Curtis. 'What ails him?'

'A slug in the shoulder. He's lost blood an' the slug is probably breeding poison in the wound.'

The young stranger nodded. 'Maybe I can help. I'm pretty good at treating wounds – anythin' like that – includin' delivering babies.'

'Jeeze – you a medico?'

'I worked with a doc for some time. You want me to attend your partner?'

Hec Redman exchanged a wary furtive glance with Harry and then nodded.

'Why not. We got nothing to lose. We want to ride out in any case an' Kid Curtis here kinda cramps our style.'

'Just give me a moment. I've got to look inside this cabin.'

Hec Redman sneered. 'If you're checkin', I can tell you your brother is real dead. Maybe you know who shot him?'

The other man nodded. 'I have a fair idea – but I'll deal with that. I want to look inside the shack.'

'Ain't nothin' there except a stinking corpse.' Hec Redman suddenly got the desire to goad this young stranger. 'You seem to have ridden a long way just to look at a dead man an' now you want to look inside the lousy cabin. Why, mister?'

'I'll answer questions when I feel like it.'

'Yeah,' Hec Redman drawled the word like an insult.

The young stranger dived inside the old shack while Harry and Redman waited, with Kid Curtis groaning on the ground. After what seemed like a long interval the young rider emerged again carrying in one hand something that seemed like a miniature totem pole. The young man looked grim, holding the wooden cylinder carefully, staring at it, then becoming aware that

Harry had fastened curious eyes on the object.

'That's a family totem,' muttered the 'breed. 'I didn't see that in the cabin.'

'Tryin' to avoid the corpse an' the stink,' jeered Hec Redman.

'Some Indian tribes keep them small totems to record their wealth an' ancestral burial grounds . . .' Harry went on slowly. 'Important to some Indian chiefs, I know.'

Hec Redman had a face like a mask. 'Yuh rode up here to git that damned little pole, didn't yuh?'

'I want to give my brother a decent burial.' The young man turned away.

'Just a lousy Injun carving!' the lean hardcase went on suspiciously.

'My brother kept it for luck.'

'Didn't bring him much, eh? You got a name, mister?'

'I'm Mark Shaw.'

'An' you know who killed your brother. I figure you're on a trail to even up an' that little totem pole has some real meanin' for you, mister.'

'You want to know the far end of a fart!' snapped Mark Shaw.

Hec Redman's fingers itched to go for his gun butt but he held back. Time to kill this ornery galoot when other things were complete.

'You figure to treat Kid Curtis – or are you all yap, stranger?'

Mark Shaw showed resentment in every sinew of his body, but he turned to the huddled wounded man and bent over him. Harry noticed that the small totem pole miniature was safely wedged in Mark Shaw's belt. Harry nursed strange little hunches in his brain concerning that carved length of wood.

For some minutes Mark Shaw was busy with the wounded Kid Curtis, turning him over, tearing the blood-soaked shirt from the shoulder and then probing the wound with a keen long-bladed knife.

Hec Redman had to hold Kid Curtis still under this treatment because the young man started to yell blue murder when the knife probed.

'I ain't seen a knife shaped like that,' said Hec.

'Surgical knife. Ain't got no other use.' Mark Shaw was quick in the circumstances, seeing that Kid Curtis twisted in agony when the knife dug into his bloody flesh and the small slug of metal was edged out. Then Mark Shaw began the process of bandaging the wound with the strips of old shirt that were provided. The shoulder was fixed up in a sling. 'He'll live.'

'Then git on your feet, Kid!' snarled Hec Redman. He grabbed at the Kid's good arm and hauled him up. 'You've ballsed us up long enough. We've got to ride out. We're headin' for Fort Worth.'

'Are you lot on the run?' asked Mark Shaw with more directness than wisdom.

'Ain't you the clever shit!' sneered Hec Redman. 'We're always on the run! And now hand over that little totem pole. I figure it's worth somethin'!'

'Only to me, mister.'

'That's your story. Your hoss an' saddle is worth plenty – an' them guns you sport.'

And suddenly the lean hardcase ruffian produced his Colt with venomous speed and stuck it in Mark Shaw's ribs. 'You're a dead man, mister!'

Hec's mistake was to take time off to gloat, to figure that he had the advantage and that the other man was as good as dead meat. The gloating process gave Mark Shaw the few seconds he needed. He jerked like a wild animal startled into instinctive reactions and his arm brushed Hec's Colt to one side, inches from his belly, which was all important because the Colt exploded flame and metal almost as fast as the young man moved. But the operative word was – *almost*!

The hot slug stung the air inches past its target and sped on its way to some useless destination. As the gun roared and Hec's finger itched for another shot, Mark Shaw slammed a jolting blow to his attacker's head. It connected and rammed the lean hardcase back. His heels dug into loose dirt and he tried to keep his balance. Mark Shaw slammed another punch into the man's guts, a process faster than drawing hardware from leather. Hec Redman rammed to the ground and gave gasping sounds as his belly contorted and vomit rose in his gullet. Mark Shaw swung around in this fragmented interval and was just in time to ram a punch at Harry. That thin man did not like violence, preferring the knife and the gun in any dangerous situation.

Harry turned, cowering, and the young man hit him savagely, showing no mercy. Then Mark Shaw knew it was time for him to get out of this risky set-up, because both men still retained guns. He swung to his horse and vaulted with the speed of a young man bred to animals, knowing his only chance of survival in this dangerous spot was to get out. Even as he hit the leather and rowelled his horse, Hec Redman got the chance to use his Colt. Lying flat on the earth he sped off another shot at this swift and ornery young galoot but the shot was too fast, badly aimed because of Hec Redman's prone position, and the bullet only cut thin air.

Mark Shaw's horse was as fast as its owner in the

risky siutation and the animal leaped away, bearing
the rider yards every passing second. As the target
moved with jerky speed, Hec and his partner Harry
loosed off some more futile Colt shots at the fleeing
horse and rider. They were out of target because hasty
gunfire and a bucking horse was not a good combina-
tion. Mark Shaw raced his animal, risking a tumble on
the broken ground, where loose stones and furrows
made speeding with a four-legged creature a bit of a
gamble. But he made it even as shots cut air all
around his body and his horse. Then he was out of the
range.

'Damn him to hell!' bawled Hec Redman. 'We could
ha' sold that hoss and the gear!'

'Yep!' Harry was still curious about the small totem
pole. He had seen a miniature like that some time in
the past and he knew that the owner prized it, but he
had forgotten why.

'Waal, damn it all, we'll head for town,' snarled Hec
Redman. 'It's all a balls but maybe we'll git lucky in
Fort Worth.'

'You figure?' lipped Harry, fed up with the other's
bossy way of dishing out orders.

'I do figure. What the hell's the matter wi' yuh?'

'I wanna eat.'

'Eat that blasted corpse in the shack!'

'You're the smart feller, huh! What about Kid Curtis
here? Ain't he gonna be a liability?'

'I'm all right,' shouted the young feller. 'That medical
feller sure got out that pesky slug. More than you lot
could do.'

'We don't give a shit if yuh live or die,' sneered Hec.

'Yeah? I'll remember that the next time yuh want
me to cover for yuh in a gun fight!'

'You die – we take your *dinero*!' Harry's voice was as cutting as a Bowie knife.

'Aw, the hell with you two. I'll be fine. Just git me on my hoss. We'll ride outa here, I take it.'

'Nothin' to stick around for.' Hec Redman's remark was full of disgust. 'We ain't goin' back to Casino Tent.'

Minutes later they were mounted and ready. As range-wide riders they should have known the recent shots carried their echoes a long way back through the thin morning air and the silent empty land. But they didn't give a damn. They didn't spend time considering niceties. Rough as all hell, they hit their saddle leather and rode out, leaving the shack and the dead body to Fate.

From a safe hiding spot Mark Shaw watched the three hardcases ride out. He cursed them grimly. He felt like killing them, then thought they weren't worth wasting slugs on. Let the bastards ride to their own hellish destiny.

He went back to the adobe shack and resolutely set about the unpleasant task of burying his dead brother. He made a shallow grave and then heaped big stones over it to stop the coyotes and other scavengers from digging for decaying flesh.

He even said a little prayer for his brother. Mark Shaw was that kind of man.

He wished he could have taken his brother back home but that seemed a bad idea now. Well, he'd given him a decent burial. And he had retrieved the miniature totem pole.

The three ruffians had not realized the value of that small carved and painted length of wood! Well, if they had known that, they'd have plugged him full of holes.

The fury of the gunshots had long died away in the

wide landscape but the sounds had not gone unnoticed. Echoes really did travel in that vast deserted land.

Kurt Kallon had heard the distant crack of the guns and he had paused and tensed, his keen hearing picking up every tiny vibration of the sounds. Guns! With men behind them!

Who were they? And why the fight? Who the blazes was shooting at who? There had been more than one gun. All handguns. Firing rather wild, he figured, being wise in all kinds of Colt-fire.

Intuition in a wild hostile terrain was almost like another pair of eyes. Or perhaps a sixth sense!

The killers he was chasing were damned sure to be involved!

SEVEN

The two girls stared inquiringly at their companion. Kurt Kallon met their eyes.

'Yeah, baddies making a lot of noise. Shootin' damned hoglegs like fire-crackers. Now who are they pot-shotting at, huh?'

'Not us, thank goodness,' answered Rose, her red hair wet from a quick wash in the cold spring water.

'I figure it's our villains from Casino Tent. So they're still helling around here.'

'Wish it was me throwing lead at them three bastards,' snapped Charity.

'My, my, you didn't learn to swear like that at the mission school,' mocked Kurt. He stamped out the camp-fire. 'Time we got after 'em!'

'You still want to kill them?' Rose searched his tanned face.

'Yup. I hate 'em.'

'Because Billy was our young friend?'

'Yeah, that and everything else.' Kurt went across to the horses and wished he had time to give them a good rub down and a decent feed of oats but that was a luxury the animals would have to do without. Time

85

was being wasted out in this wilderness of silence and vast spaces.

It was time for action. That meant shooting action. And he did not forget that the crooked Carl Rigg was out there somewhere with a greed for the dead men's gold. Sure as hell he would have heard those distant cracks of Colt fire.

Carl Rigg, huh! Yeah, another twister who had his eyes on gold and little concern for his duty as sheriff. It sure figured that Rigg had been as devious as any crook he'd ever tried to lock up!

'We got to start scouting around,' stated Kurt. 'We got to sight those hellions an' get this business over.'

Rose looked troubled. Her eyes were downcast. 'I sometimes wish we could let the law deal with it.'

'No evidence. Well, nothing that an honest judge would spend time on. And those rannigans are travelling men and would be out of this territory in weeks – maybe headin' for California or the Yukon for all we might know.'

'Well, we're not going to forget they killed Billy, murdered him, in fact,' Charity went on. She looked really feminine with her blonde hair blowing around her face in the slight breeze that came up the valley.

'Get to your horses,' said Kurt quietly. 'We're going after them, unless you want to return to Cragside.'

'Without firing a shot?' exclaimed Rose. 'An' I mean a shot at those three brutes.'

'Brutes now – not bastards!' joked Kurt.

'Charity called them bastards,' said Rose. 'And I agree with her.'

'You two always agree,' countered Kurt. 'Even to sharing me.'

'That won't last!'

'Ah! You got a galoot in sight?'

'You ain't the only feller with long legs and a broad hairy chest in this wide, wide world.'

In time they were on their horses, cinches tightened and rein-leathers in hand. Slowly the three made a way out from their temporary camp; the fire was dead and most signs of their brief presence were gone.

The horses picked a slow way over rock-strewn ground, the three riders sitting silent for the time being. Random thoughts filled their heads. There were a few doubts; a few uncertain feelings, especially in the minds of the girls. In the final analysis, they knew they relied on Kurt.

Sure they could kill if the moment of truth arrived. If it so happened that they met up with the killers, they could shoot, unless the men got a few slugs in first! There was always that chance. They were chasing killers in deadly earnest, not good-looking galoots on a dance floor!

Kurt wished he had some clues as to the hell-bents. The distant cracks of Colt-fire had given a tiny sense of direction at the time but all that was fading and the vast land just swallowed up everything.

He headed the animals for some low hills to the north, looking for sign all the way, which was in fact like looking for needles in a haystack. With tight lips and a feeling of futility he got Big Feller to the crest of a hill, the girls just behind him. He pulled his hat down a bit, shading his eyes from the morning sun and stared grimly all around the terrain. Big country, broken, too, where men and animals could hide or even ride down deep defiles.

All at once he spotted the distant rider. Kurt sat tall in the saddle and stared.

'Man ahead, girls.'

'One man?' Rose joined him.

'Yeah. One galoot. Long way off but we can catch up with him because he ain't in any hurry.'

'We're lookin' for three men,' snapped Charity.

'Sure. But it don't do any harm to talk to a man out here in this empty land.'

'What might he be doing riding out here? Can we trust strangers?'

Kurt patted his holstered Peacemaker. 'I can.'

Rose and Charity gave little laughs. 'You're a gunny, ain't you, Kurt? You always put your trust in hardware.'

'An' you two pards,' he countered. 'Next to my gun, I love you two.'

Rose giggled. 'I'll remember that the next time we're in a real bed.'

The three riders hustled the horses along over the rocky going interspersed with grass and sand as the sun warmed the land. Kurt felt sweat on the back of his neck. He also felt damned hungry. God, they hadn't eaten real grub like steak for what seemed ages! For a moment civilization and an eating house seemed like a distant paradise.

And then they were almost on the man. He turned his animal and faced them. His gun appeared like magic in a capable fist.

'We come in peace, feller, as the Indians would say,' Kurt made it sound like a joke. 'Put that hogleg away.'

'I will, seein' you've got two ladies with you – although I ain't seen wimmen wearing pants for a long time.'

'We ain't no ladies,' laughed Charity.

'Surely?' The young man waited.

'We're chasing some men, real bad hats,' yapped Charity, pushing a blonde curl back under her Stetson.

'Actually, we're always chasing men,' added Rose, not to be outdone by her sidekick. 'But these three are pigs.'

Mark Shaw slowly shoved his gun back in holster leather. 'Yeah? Maybe I can help?'

'Three thugs, one a 'breed kind of galoot,' said Kurt.

'Yeah, an' one wounded, a youngish guy?'

Kurt stared. 'You know?'

'Met up with them, back at the adobe hut.'

'Yuh didn't git any kind of grief with them?'

Mark Shaw laughed. 'Sure did.'

'You exchanged some shots? Was it you throwing off lead?'

'More like those three tried to salivate me an' my horse. Yeah they did try to gun me down.'

'An' you got away?' Kurt eyed the young man with interest. He saw clean-cut features, a certain amount of beard stubble and concluded that this stranger was usually clean-shaven, not always a habit in the frontier lands and towns.

'Yeah, I got away an' I'm heading for home.'

'Where might that be, friend?'

'Way past Fort Worth. You sure seem mighty curious.'

Kurt laughed. 'Just habit. You know how it is. We're out of Cragside. I figure the killers we're after might head for Fort Worth too, because a town like that is good to hell around in.'

As the party slowly rode down the long valley, which was part of the undulating terrain leading to the hills around Fort Worth, Kurt noticed that the two girls were eyeing Mark Shaw with that kind of interest that always showed in their eyes when a personable male came their way. Well, Rose Merit and Charity Brendan were free agents! Even so, Kurt was aware that he resented any man who took too much interest in the girls. He knew that was crazy. He had no hold on them. He hadn't ever proposed to one of them. All right, so they had shared beds! But that had been a natural thing, it had seemed, at the time of bedding.

As they picked an easy way down the rock-strewn slope, with the sun bright on the distant bluish hills, Charity fluffed out her blonde hair, where it showed from under her hat, and got to talking animatedly to the young galoot. This was so obviously the sexual fascination of a girl for a guy, and with Charity, pretty blatant!

'You married, mister?'

'Nope. Too much work to do.'

'What work?'

'I got a small spread.'

'And no wife to do the chores?' Charity giggled her way through the questions and Kurt felt like spitting.

'An oldster helps me out.'

'Ain't the same as a woman, huh? What's your name, mister?'

'Mark Shaw. What's yours?'

'I'm Charity – an' this is my pal Rose. An' this tall feller is Kurt Kallon an' he looks after us, so don't you get too sassy with me or Rose or he'll be after yuh.'

'I'll bear that in mind.' Mark Shaw smiled his interest in the shapely Charity and made little attempt to hide the gleam in his eyes.

Kurt, the two girls and the young man, made a definite presence in the bright light as they allowed the animals to pick a careful way down the slope. With the sun on them, and the sound of their voices, particularly of the girls' as they laughed loudly, they were noticed. It was strange how, in a barren landscape, people converged.

A stocky man in a tweed jacket and a worn hat pulled down low heard the party make their way. Horses kicked at loose stones. The hooves made noises. Added to those were the humans yelling remarks at each other.

The man, still sporting a sheriff's badge, edged deeper into a thorn bush that overhung a cleft in the yellow-soil cliff-edge. He saw Kurt's party clearly but he was unobserved. Carl Rigg always figured he had the luck.

So there was the ornery bastard with the gold in the canvas bag. With him were the two girls, fresh as all hell, damn them! But who was the newcomer, the jasper in the good-quality range clothes and the guns to suit? Yeah, a holstered Colt and a rifle in the saddle scabbard. Seemed like this silent empty land had a quality for attracting strangers!

Carl Rigg watched them, congratulating himself that he had at least found the tall hell-bent without trouble.

He figured it needed only chance and one shot to get his hands on that poke full of gold dust and chips. Then, a fast ride to God knows where as long as there was an assayer's office nearby who would buy the gold, and he could consign his badge to the blasted desert and keep on riding.

Carl Rigg watched Kurt and the others disappear slowly into the distance. Then he carefully emerged from his hiding-place.

Kurt was looking for sign of any riders who might

have lately gone along these trails. He found little to encourage him. But he figured the three men who had murdered Billy were somewhere along these silent routes to Fort Worth.

Like some signal in the silent wastland air, a solitary rifle shot rang out and disturbed some birds, all of which seemed to be about a mile away. Kurt and his party pulled up while Kurt rose tall in his stirrups and stared around him.

'Now who would that be?' he muttered. 'One damned shot!'

'Wasn't a hand-gun,' commented Mark Shaw.

Nothing moved except the distant birds and to Kurt Kallon they marked the spot. 'Some character out there.'

'Just one man?' asked Rose. 'We're searching for three.'

'Yeah . . . don't know why he fired a rifle but I think I'll find out. You lot stick around.'

'I'll ride with you.' Mark Shaw seemed ready to help.

'Stick with the girls, *amigo*. That's safer. Rose – Charity – fill in Mark about the killers we're huntin'.'

'I got a good idea when I rode like hell away from them.'

'Yeah, but the girls will tell you in detail about their brother, Billy, just to give you an idea.'

Without another wasted word, Kurt rowelled his big horse and made him leap into full stride down the hill. The girls watched him go with mixed feelings.

'Well, at least we're not without a man to hand!' snapped Rose.

Mark Shaw smiled. The girls suddenly got the notion that this young feller liked the ladies, as if they needed telling.

Kurt Kallon urged Big Feller on, down the thorn-bush trail, across open land when he found it and then around a large butte that was a landmark in the terrain. He covered a fair distance at speed, with Big Feller kicking up a cloud of dust. Then he decided to slow his approach. He could be riding into danger. Well, if the grief was the three killers, he'd welcome that.

His impetuousness brought him to the three men and the grief, sure thing! As he went down a shallow gully at full lope, he distinctly saw the three riders way out on the flat land, close to a clump of scrub timber trees. One man was holding up a dead range turkey, recently killed, it seemed. So that was the reason for the one rifle shot.

Kurt knew the three were the lousy killers. One was the grim-faced man in dirty range gear, his pants covered in dust and his face dark with beard, and the other was a 'breed, a man in a tall hat, and his thick shirt decorated with snakeskin. The third was the young man whose arm was held in a rough sling made out of some torn shirt. They were the men as described by Mark Shaw in the brief account he'd given, but Kurt also knew these were the dirty killers he'd set out to get, the men who had murdered Billy.

Kurt drew in his horse but his onward rush had been a bit too fast, with Big Feller kicking hell out of the terrain, and the three men ahead on the flattish stretch of ground whipped around as the hooves thundered toward them.

Handguns were whipped out and shots cracked the air. The three gunnies did not need to be told that here was an enemy. Hec Redman was the first to throw random lead from his gun and Harry, the 'breed, followed his example, throwing shots like mad. Kid

Curtis was a bit handicapped because he could only use his left hand and his Colt .45 was too secure in his right-hand holster but he did manage to blast off some shots at the oncoming horseman.

Kurt paid the penalty of his unusual lack of caution. A shot hissed through the air and plugged him in his shoulder. He jerked with the pain and tumbled helplessly from the saddle. He hit the earth with such force that he was momentarily stunned.

EIGHT

'We've been trailin' you lousy murderous skunks for ages!' yelled Kurt Kallon, the effort of shouting making agony streak through his bloodied wound. He put a hand to his shoulder as if to ease the pain as he lay under the scrub timber. He glared at the three men as they laughed their vicious enjoyment of the situation. They stood over him, hands on hips. Only one man had a gun in his fist and that was Hec Redman. They had dragged Kurt to the shade of the trees, not for humanitarian reasons but because it seemed a place to stop and question their prisoner. Kurt's big horse stood nearby, ears pricking, the reins dangling.

'Finish him off,' suggested Kid Curtis, his young face devoid of any compassion. 'What are yuh waitin' for, Hec?'

'Let the long bastard talk.'

'Suit yourself.' The Kid shrugged, plucked at a long grass and began to chew on the stalk. 'What the hell good will that do? You heard him. He's been after us.'

'You been down to Casino Tent?' Hec Redman just felt he had to know the full score before he blew this galoot away.

95

'Yeah. You were down there, in that valley, weren't yuh?'

'Yup. Figured to pick up some money but all that happened was some ginks got shot.'

Kurt nodded. 'That young shit one of them, huh?' He nodded at Kid Curtis. That young man started forward and kicked at Kurt Kallon as he lay on the ground. Kurt tried to soak up the pain and stifle a groan. His shoulder hurt like mad. He knew he was in a damned fix. God, he'd rode down on these men like a fool!

'You're the dirt who killed Billy,' he muttered, playing for time as much as anything.

'Billy? Now who the hell is Billy?' Hec Redman spat dust out of his parched throat, dirt and saliva mixed with phlegm, the filth seeming to indicate his nature.

'You don't remember? You shot him – you and your pals – in a card-game and took the winnings.'

'Did we?' Hec Redman grinned at Harry. The latter stared, his lined face a mask of dust and hawk-like features. 'So what!'

'Ain't the first jasper we put down,' sneered Kid Curtis. 'You figure we got to remember 'em all?'

Hec Redman might be a villainous lout but he had the natural cunning of his kind. 'You said we. That means more than one.'

'Did I?' Kurt felt the blood ooze from his wound.

'You said *we've* been trailin'! We! Not just you, mister.'

'The slug in my shoulder hurts like blazes. I don't know what I said.' Swiftly, Kurt realized he had to put these men off the trail to the girls.

'I figure you got pards, mister.' Hec Redman kicked Kurt again. 'Now talk. Who are yuh with? You ain't alone.'

'Yeah?'

Hec began to smile. 'Sure we took the winnings. Jest kiddin' you along, you tall shit! You think you can fool with us? Better jaspers than you have tried that trick.'

Kurt felt trapped. It began to dawn on him that he'd end up real dead. Then who would look after Charity and Rose? Well, of course, at the moment they were with Mark Shaw.

He remained silent and then there was a twist to the chain of events. Kid Curtis gave a shout. He had been close to Kurt's big horse, admiring the tough haunches, and then he got around to looking in Kurt's saddle-bags. 'Jeeze! Look what we got?'

'What the hell are you yappin' about, Kid?' Hec was feeling like shooting his victim right there and then.

'Gold!' The Kid's yell rang out.

'Are yuh crazy?'

'I tell yuh – gold in this canvas poke!'

The effect was instantaneous. The three hellions began to crowd around Kid Curtis as he held the small poke up for the others to see. Hec Redman carefully dipped a wet finger into the poke and when he brought it out again he could see the tiny glinting particles which he instinctively knew was the precious metal men would kill to obtain.

Kurt was ignored. He stared at the three killers as they crowded together. It was now or never because if he just lay still with the painful wound he'd be dead in another five minutes.

He rose silently to his feet, agony jagging through his flesh, and crept softly away as the three hardcases began to talk excitedly among themselves.

He moved like a shadow, five paces away, and then another two. The three ruffians were still touching the poke, talking crazily to each other, almost yelling their greedy excitement. Gold did that to hard men! Gold fever! Many men had died for the dust and the nuggets.

Kurt got away, softly, yards at a time, blessing his luck. He had to get up to Big Feller. He wouldn't get far without the animal and its strong legs.

Another yard and he was touching the hide of the big horse. Would his luck hold? It damned-well had to!

They were so taken up with the prospect of gold, something these hard men had always dreamed about finding, that they lost all sense of their surroundings and the man they had left in blood on the ground.

Kurt reached up for the saddlehorn. He gripped hard. He then whipped a leg across the saddle. His backside was flat on the leather. Time to get to hell out of it!

He did just that. Incredibly the three baddies were still lost in the fascination of gold. They only turned round when Big Feller's hooves thudded into the earth.

'Jeeze! He's hittin' the trail!'

Guns flashed to dirty paws but as Big Feller raced into a full gallop, Kurt sank low on the horse's back. He knew the three men would wise up to him in seconds. And then that meant slugs!

Luck smiled on Kurt in the next few blazing seconds of furious activity. He got Big Feller into full stride before the first shot blazed through the air.

Crack! Crack! Big Feller's hooves rammed the earth. Then: Crack! Crack!

The slugs tore air but they did not hit Kurt's flesh. His horse, too, escaped a bullet although it was a large target. The beast jerked and twisted as forelegs and haunches rammed madly at the ground.

And then Kurt was racing away, torn with pain in his shoulder but blessing his luck at his escape.

He rowelled the animal hard. The space between horse and man and the hellions increased, then Kurt jerked the animal round a red-stone crag and really got away. Big Feller headed out, anywhere, like his rider instinctively glad to escape.

Kurt Kallon was in the clear. He realized the shooting would be heard for miles around in the silent land.

And that was true. A man called Carl Rigg heard the gunshot commotion and froze, pressing back against a cliff. Gunnies! More than one hogleg judging by the sounds!

Then Kurt was a long way off. Hec Redman and his two sidekicks could have jumped to saddles but they were still mesmerized by the canvas poke of gold. Already they knew there was weight there – and that meant wealth! They watched Kurt go. They holstered guns.

'The hell wi' that jasper!'

'Are yuh goin' to let him hit the trail?' Harry's lined face, the colour of leather, jerked a wary glance at the fleeing horseman, but even his impassive nature was aroused by the sight of gold. 'Jeeze! Gold! It's paydirt! We can buy anything!'

'Yeah!' Hec Redman agreed but inwardly thought: *Do we have to share it?*

Kid Curtis was full of young excitement. 'Gold. Goddamn it! Now who would have figured that jasper was loaded with gold?'

'We're rich!' cackled Hec Redman. 'It's a gift! Durn me!'

'We could still catch up with that cuss,' Harry grated. 'Maybe find out where he got the gold.'

'Aw, damn him.' Hec Redman was holding the canvas poke, weighing it in his hand and mentally assessing the value of this startling find. Even he was not disposed to rough-ride over the land just to shoot up a man. The gink was wounded. Maybe he'd fall from his big horse and break his neck. There were a lot of maybes!

In actual fact Kurt Kallon was hanging on to his horse by sheer will power and riding ability because his senses swam as the hooves pounded the land and he lay close to Big Feller's mane, clinging on for dear life. Then his brain thought clearly again and he headed the animal in the right direction. He knew he had to get back to the two girls. Nausea flooded him. He was hardly aware at times of where the horse was taking him, and Big Feller knew that something was wrong and in momentary fright changed direction twice.

But the animal had sure instincts. It raced up a shale slope and galloped straight for the thorn-filled gully where Rose and Charity sat their horses and waited with Mark Shaw for Kurt's return.

Sure the sound of the gunfire had reached them but they hardly knew where to ride out to. And then they heard the sound of hoof-beats on dry ground and within minutes Kurt was in sight. Mark Shaw swiftly rode up to Big Feller and slowed the animal's pace, grabbing the leathers. Then Kurt slowly rolled from his saddle and hit the ground. The girls leaned over him.

Charity shrieked: 'Blood! Kurt – are you all right?'

'You silly bitch – he's been plugged in the shoulder!' Rose turned on her sister. 'It's those killers!'

Mark Shaw was the one with the practical medical skill and the next ten minutes were spent in making

Kurt comfortable while the young man searched his saddle-bag for his surgical knives.

'Hell! Seems I'm getting plenty of practice at digging out slugs way out here in the wild!'

Charity moved agitatedly, hefting her gun and look-ing wildly around at the semi-desert landscape 'I want to kill those men. First Billy – and now Kurt.'

'He ain't dead!' snapped Rose.

'Not by a long chalk,' added Mark Shaw. 'But I've got to stop the loss of blood. And the slug has to come out.'

A long way off a man crept silent as an Indian tracker, taking advantage of all cover in this broken land. He had left his horse ground-hitched way back because animals were hefty creatures and made noise. He crawled and sidled to the spot where the three men stood with their animals and yelled gloating remarks about gold. Carl Rigg even saw one man hold up the canvas poke in some sort of boastful triumph and yell for the tenth time. 'Gold, by Jesus!'

Carl Rigg knew he was taking risks. These hard-cases were gunnies with plenty of cunning experience of hard trails and dangerous men. They'd gunned down the long galoot, only for him to make good his escape by pure chance. Carl Rigg had seen the rider escape even though slugs had cut the air from many direc-tions. The man had been relieved of his poke of gold, damn it all! Maybe that was a bad change. The three other hellbents knew about the gold, and in fact they had it in their possession. Hell, how would he ever get his hands on that passel o' gold now that three hard bastards had it in their dirty paws? Aw, Goddamn it!

Christ, he'd have to trail 'em! And keep silent as a snake. Three ornery devils. Range rats as sure as hell.

Mark Shaw had the skill of a trained doctor

although his training had been acquired the rough and ready way. Soon he had Kurt snug on a blanket, near some shelter provided by a large rock, the deadly piece of metal dug from bleeding flesh by his expert hands and his collection of strangely-shaped knives. Kurt was conscious. He muttered some thanks.

'Good thing you're around, *amigo*.'

'You'll have to stay still for some time.'

'Those three villains!'

'They'll have to wait.'

'They've got the gold.'

'What gold?'

Kurt grunted and managed a smile. He then told Mark Shaw about the gold and the two scallywags, Dad Bowker and Snap. 'They robbed a prospector of that gold. Dangerous stuff is the yellow metal. Now the killers have it. Aw, I'll tell you the whole yarn.'

So for some time the two men conversed, with Kurt going back in time to tell Mark Shaw the full details as to how Billy Graham had been killed and robbed.

The two girls lit a fire and prepared some food although the rations in their saddle-bags were low.

'Aw, damn, we should be goin' after those killer galoots!' snapped Kurt. 'And here I am brought down by a slug.'

'You'll be all right.'

'You'll be fine, given another day or so,' said Rose.

'We should be riding.'

'It can wait.'

As time went on and they made a rough camp, Kurt was aware that Mark Shaw spent a lot of time just staring at the two girls even when he was supposedly busy with other chores, such as rubbing the dust out of the animals' hides. When Rose bent over the camp-fire and a cook-pot, the young man stared damned hard at her rounded behind. Sure, tightly stretched trousers were a temptation for any horny galoot and Kurt was begining to realize that Mark Shaw was just that.

Kurt was restless. Even if he was wounded, lying around was not to his liking, not when the itch to salivate the three hardcase killers smouldered in his being.

'We got to git after them. They got the damned gold! They killed Billy – an' I ain't gonna let 'em git away with that.'

'Taking the law into your own hands?' Mark Shaw stood near Kurt and stared reflectively.

'There ain't no law out here.'

'There is in Fort Worth. A man called Jake Duerr don't stand for killing, so I hear.'

Charity came over to Mark Shaw. 'I want those three bastards dead!' She snapped the statement out mercilessly.

'You wouldn't shoot them in cold blood?'

'I'd give 'em a chance to equal me in a draw!' yelled the girl, her blonde hair swirling as she jerked her head angrily.

'You? Equal three men – hard case gunnies?'

'A slug from my gun is as fast as a slug from one of theirs.'

Mark Shaw grinned. He slid an arm around the girl's waist and held her tightly, his fingers smoothing into flesh around her hips. He boldly challenged her, in an intimate way, and Kurt Kallon saw the bawdy play and knew again that Mark Shaw was encroaching on territory that he had thought for a long time was his. Damn the young man! He was a woman-lover, no doubt. And he didn't care that Kurt saw him making his play. Kurt scowled, lying back, his wound giving him momentary hell. In that moment, staring at Mark Shaw, seeing him caressing Charity, he disliked the young buckaroo.

Then Kurt cursed himself. He didn't own Charity!

The same situation happened an hour later, after they'd shot a large rattler and decapitated the reptile, and Rose had shown Mark Shaw how to make a stew with the flesh. 'It's good stuff. Ain't you eaten snake stew with wild corn?'

'No! Where in tarnation did you learn to cook that kinda thing?'

'Out in the wilds – with Kurt. It's food, damn yuh!'

'Yeah, but – I sure prefer steak, the best, off the rump. Like I prefer rump in other ways!'

And the red-blooded galoot slid a hand around Rose's ample hip and gave her more than a hug. His hands were definitely exploratory. And, from Kurt's angry point of view, the girl seemed to like the touch! She wriggled a bit, smiled into Mark Shaw's tanned face and showed little inclination to slip out of his embrace.

Kurt turned his face away. Fuming, he felt like going up to the young bucko and slamming a punch into his visage. Then Kurt knew this was crazy. He didn't own Rose and her body any more than he owned Charity! And he knew damned well he couldn't punch a paper bag at this moment without giving his wound hell and making the blood flow again.

The hours wore on. The sun was heading downwards. The air would become cooler and then night would fall. And all they were doing was wasting time. Suddenly, as they all sat around the fire eating, he bawled at the top of his voice, 'Aw, the hell with this!

Those killers are gettin' clear to hell away!'

'We can't ride after them,' said Mark Shaw. 'You'd lose a lot of blood and probably fall off your hoss.'

'Oh, would I? Well, as I remember things, that young gun-hand with the other killer thugs is handicapped the same way with a shoulder wound – an' it ain't stopped him – an' they are getting away with that damned gold!'

'Is it just that gold you're concerned about?' Charity flung the challenge at Kurt.

'Aw, the hell with yuh, gal. You know I want those rats dead for Billy's sake.'

Charity almost made her next comment sound like a feminine sneer. 'Well, you ain't gonna get within shootin' distance just lying there.'

Kurt leaped up, his legs buckling for a moment as pain from his shoulder wound streaked through him.

'Goddamn the lot of yuh! Let's git backsides to leather an' ride!'

'What, now? The sun will be down in an hour.'

'Then we'll be an hour nearer those three ranni-gans.'

He was mad as all hell. Actually, the thought of the three hellions escaping with the gold wasn't the prime reason for his fury. He was angry at the way Mark Shaw used every opportunity to fondle the girls. The galoot seemed unable to resist patting a jean-clad buttock or inching a hand around a shapely waist.

'You could fall from your horse,' Mark Shaw reminded him.

'I ain't some jasper who's never sat anything harder than an office chair!' yelled Kurt. His long legs took him over to the other man and they stared hard at each other.

'What are you so riled about?' Mark Shaw smiled from under his near-new Stetson because he knew full well the forthcoming answer.

'You – blast your hide!'

'Me? What have I done, friend?'

'You been pawing my two gals!'

'Your two gals? Jeeze, man, the chapels say a guy is entitled to take only one girl as a wife.'

Kurt prodded the other young man's chest with a long hard finger. 'I ain't married – an' Charity an' Rose are kinda – wal – both my friends.'

Mark Shaw grinned. 'You ain't married to one o' them.'

'That sure is right!' screamed the girls almost simultaneously.

Then Rose added: 'He don't own me! I pick my own kind of lovin' man.'

'Me, too,' yelled Charity. She giggled and flung a glance at Mark Shaw and then moved indecisively around the camp-fire.

Mark Shaw lost his grin. 'You're still proddin' my chest, friend!'

'Yeah? Wal, I aim to take a poke at yuh, too.' And Kurt swung his fist at the other man's visage, so invitingly close to him.

Pain tore fiendishly through Kurt's wounded flesh although he was using his free right hand, the other arm being in a sling. His fist connected with Mark Shaw's chin but it lacked any real force and the young guy merely jerked his head away. Still, anger glinted in his eyes. He instinctively squared up to Kurt, fists raised. But he did not fling a punch.

'Go ahead, damn yuh! Hit me!' yelled Kurt Kallon and he flung another blow at the other man. The fist

rammed into Mark Shaw's cheek and hurt Kurt more
than it hurt the other. Mark Shaw stepped away, backing. His fists were raised and his eyes glared defiance
at Kurt. The two girls crowded around, amusement
drained from their pretty faces. Charity yelled: 'Stop it,
you two!'

Even to move his shoulder gave Kurt streaking pain
but it was the kind of hurt he had had to put up with
in many a long trail ride – and in many a fight – and
he swung again at the other man. The blow missed
Mark Shaw's face and slid over his shoulder, bringing
the two furious young men close to each other where
for some seconds they glared hell at each other.

Then Kurt felt a hard gun barrel ram into his side
and a voice hiss: 'Cut it out!'

NINE

Darkness blacked the earth with only a faint halo of moonlight creeping through the cumulus and casting some light over the camp scene. The red flames from a good crackling blaze added to the illumination in that immediate circle, defining the three sprawling hard-cases like the menacing creatures they were. Hec Redman looked like a black animal, wary, watching, the gold in the canvas poke secured around his pants belt, his Colt a hard reminder of the equally hard life around him. Harry, the 'breed, lay motionless, his hat low down on his forehead, his eyes barely visible. But they were snakelike and wary, hiding his thoughts. Only Kid Curtis made noises.

'Aw, hell – wish we were in Fort Worth! This damned wound is bleeding again. That jasper didn't help me much.'

'Quit your goddamned moaning, you young crap-head. He got the damned slug out of your carcase.'

'Yeah – but I'm bleedin'. I need a new bandage. I feel kinda sick. We should ha' been in town by now where they got real docs.'

'An' a nosy town marshal, I hear.' Hec Redman touched his gun. He thought: One blasted slug will stop

109

your goddamned belly-achin' for good, you young
bastard!

Harry's black eyes flicked from side to side. He
thought: He's hanging on to that gold, sure thing. Ain't
never once said a pesky word about sharing it out!

Beyond the flickering flames of the fire, out in the
dark and cold night air, a man in a thick jacket crawled
into the rock crevice and watched and waited. His thick
tweed jacket helped keep out the night air but tedium
was creeping into his bones. Maybe he should get to
hell away from this. One wrong move – a sneeze in the
silent night – and he'd be a dead man.

But the thought of the gold mesmerized Carl Rigg
and kept him silently watching, like some creature
waiting for its prey to make a false move. He realized
he could not jump the three hard men, even if one was
handicapped by a wound, but he hated the thought of
moving away. Gold! One of these rannigans had it, and
probably that was the leader, the sinister hardcase, the
one who gave the orders. Now if the man fell asleep, as
could be expected, maybe the gold might be within
reach. Even hard cusses had to sleep.

Carl Rigg waited.

Another waiting man was Harry, his inner thoughts
full of wary suspicion, as always because he was an
individual who had lived all his life watching other
men, knowing their hands were almost always against
him, his skin and aquiline features inviting antagonism. From his earliest days as a boy he'd had to
distrust the human animals around him because he
was 'breed and expected to be a cunning rat. He'd been
kicked around the ranch-town where he'd lived as a
boy. White men sneered at him and kicked him out of
their way and in his first job he'd had to work like a

slave from morn till night and then be spat on. All men, he figured, were shit. He'd discovered long ago that a man with a slug in the guts couldn't do him much harm. He had learnt that when he was seventeen, when he'd pumped slugs into a white man piss-happy with his own importance. Of course he'd had to take to the owl hoot trail and, in fact, had been on it ever since.

He figured he could be rich – if the gold in the canvas poke belonged to him and no one else. Why should he share it with a white bastard like Hec Redman, or the crazy Kid Curtis?

Harry rose silently to his feet, his lean frame another shadow around the camp-fire, and he stood thinking grimly and impassively as he looked down at the two sleeping men.

Hell, they were trusting fools, or was it mere fatigue? Probably both were partly true because even the hardest cuss had to close his eyes some time and trust to the others around him and to fate. Harry drew his gun very slowly, standing like a direful sentinel over the two sleeping men. He could kill them with swift shots, pumping the lethal lead into flesh and blood. Then he'd be rich, for the price of two bits of vicious metal. They wouldn't be able to trail him because dead galoots can't sit saddles. He could get clear to hell away with the murders. Murder! Now who the heck gave a shit about murder? A man was either alive in the world, eating, screwing, drinking, or he was just meat for the coyotes. Murder was just a word.

As Harry tensed, wondering, strangely unsure of events although his finger itched to squeeze the trigger of the long heavy Colt, he heard a tiny alien sound in the night, just beyond the thickest shroud of blackness.

Harry turned slowly, his Indian blood colouring all his suspicions, adding to his wary instincts about the wild just beyond him. A man had made that little scraping noise!

Harry stepped away from the fire quickly and then paused again. His body was stiff, every sinew hard. All his senses were tuned, as if he would read something from even a whisper in the cool night air. Then he heard the odd sound again.

This time he recognized the little noise. Some jasper was dragging a boot over rock, thinking he was as silent as a shadow. Well, it was a damn good imitation but a scraping boot wasn't a natural part of the night.

His inner tension turning him into a hunting animal, his ancestry urging him to be the solitary man, Harry went into the night air, where even the fitful moonlight barely reached. With a gun in hand, he felt the real hunter. He'd kill whatever was out there. He'd do it because he felt it was natural to hunt. All his killer instincts were aroused, creeping through his blood like maggots.

As Harry went into the night's black shroud, Hec Redman's hand moved under the grey horse-blanket. His eyes opened, narrowed and filled with anger as they cut the gloom. The blanket undulated as if a rat was hidden there. Then Hec's hand pushed through. The big gun was unveiled.

Hec pulled his battered hat down, got to his feet. His guts churned. It wasn't just bile mixed with hate. His gut was full of crappy food hardly fit for a mangy dog. He was sour. He knew he had been within a minute of bloody death, if he'd been unable to beat the 'breed to an avenging slug. Equalizing was a tricky game. They could both have died.

What in hell was Harry doing out there in the night?

The 'breed's boots slowly padded through the grass and clutching creeper, past where the horses lay resting. He went on slowly, gun poking the night like a menace. Harry knew there was a man out there. He could feel it in his blood. He thought he could even smell a guy. But that was sure just hunter's brain reaching out.

Harry's legs went on, one stride after the other, so slowly it was almost action in slow motion. Then he saw the dark shape, blacker than the night, a man knowing he was being trailed and rising to his feet for a desperate dash. The shape could have been anything in the night, darting through wild thorn bush. The shape even looked like a ghostie, a phantom of the silent black air, but Harry knew the rustling, fleeing mass for a prowling man and he fired his hogleg with trained speed.

The blast of shells shattered the night just as the fatal slug hacked into the other man's body and sent him sprawling in a death dive.

Hec Redman and the Kid were on their feet. The horses hauled their bodies up on nervous legs, their sinews taut. Hec and Kid Curtis lurched through the blackness, fists clamped around shooting irons.

It seemed natural for the men to yell curses and questions into the night air and even as they bawled angrily the cloud swirled silently away as if wanting to reveal the scene. Somewhere the quarter moon shed light.

'Jeeze – who is he?' Hec Redman rammed up to Harry and stared down at the bleeding corpse.

'Don't yuh know?'

'He's a goddamned dead man – that's all!'

'Nope. He's the flamin' badge-toter! The blasted sheriff outa Cragside.'

Hec Redman turned the body with his boot. 'Yeah! Hell's bells! He's been trailin' us.'

He stared at the badge pinned to Carl Rigg's checked shirt. Strangely, the man had put his badge back, as if reluctant to disown himself from his former office in life.

Hec Redman kicked the body. Blood pumped from the deep wounds in the man's chest where Harry's slugs had effectively torn his heart.

'Trailin' us! Well, he's one dead man.'

Some deep-rooted instinct told Harry that the man had smelled gold and known they were carrying the fateful canvas poke. Gold had a way of scenting the air, of stretching the nerves of men to the point where they could sense motives and discover clues to the metal that brought death more than it brought happiness.

'How'd yuh know he was out here?' Hec Redman figured to kid the 'breed along.

'I heard sounds.'

'Don't yuh ever flamin' sleep, Harry?'

'Yep. I sleep.' Harry pulled his hat down so low it almost covered his nose.

Hec Redman hefted his belt. The bag of gold seemed reassuringly heavy.

Hec grinned sneeringly. 'Some blasted day you'll hit the long sleep, Harry. You'll be dead – or do you figure to live for ever?'

'What the hell are yuh gettin' at?'

Hec Redman could have told the half-Indian that he'd had a Colt aimed at him from under the blanket and that he'd been a second away from death while he hesitated about killing. Come to think of it, maybe they'd both been moments away from death. Nervy hands weren't always accurate.

Hec turned away and patted the gold-weighted poke near his belt. He had one sardonic thought. Maybe the gold would kill him!

Kid Curtis stamped back to the smouldering fire. 'Aw, hell, we should be in Fort Worth. This life ain't worth a crap!'

The night meant sleep for most people and for animals, and Kurt's party hugging a hollow miles away among rocks and sheltering bluffs was no different. Kurt had told Charity Brendan: 'The next time you stick your gun into my side might be your last move, dear lady.'

'I had to stop you two fighting.'

'What if I'd whipped out my gun and fired?'

'At me? You knew it was me behind yuh!'

They had covered some miles before the darkness and the rough terrain forced them to stop and the feud between Kurt and Mark Shaw had simmered down into a steady dislike of each other. It wasn't the first time in human history that pretty women had come between two sane men.

Kurt felt he couldn't compare with Mark Shaw, on account of his shoulder wound and that riled him. And he'd been bested by the three killers over the poke of gold. Those skunks had the gold. This trail ride for Billy's killers was coming unstuck. Things were not adding up right.

There was still animosity.

'You could ride on, Mr Shaw. We don't need yuh to find them blasted murderers. They ain't that far away in this damned wilderness and I'll get them.'

'With one gammy arm? Wal, sure thing you got a good right hand and arm.'

'Good enough to use a Peacemaker. An' good enough to hang one on yuh, mister!'

Mark Shaw merely grinned. And that night added to Kurt's dislike of the young bucko, for an hour later, when the fire had burnt down to a reddish glow, he found Charity and Martin Shaw sleeping together under blankets and so close they were as one body. Anger rising in him like a sullen thing, Kurt sidled over to Rose, moved her blanket and gently nestled close to her. Her eyes opened. Long lashes flicked at him.

'So you come to me when you can't get Charity?'

'Don't talk like that. Yuh know it ain't like that.'

'What is it like, Kurt?'

'Give me a kiss, dammit. I need some consolation. That damned bucko is bestin' me.' His mouth hunted for her lips and he drew her really close so that their bodies blended although the clothes they wore stopped skin from meeting skin. 'Rose – Rose – yuh know I really like you.'

'Like?'

'Yeah. Sure I like – wal, hell, I love yuh.'

'You've said that to Charity,' she mocked.

'How in tarnation do you know that?'

'She has told me, you fool. Come here – closer, damn yuh. Git that goddamned belt off! Gee, you smell of horse! And that sling around your shoulder sure gets in the way.'

In the gloom, Kurt smiled. 'I can slip out o' that – an' other things. I ain't useless.' And he proceeded to prove the statement and his manhood.

Many hours later when the sun rose and warmed

the earth and sent some distant birds soaring into the morning sky, they got up and rubbed sleep from their eyes, washed in the spring water and made a fire so that they could at least have hot coffee in which to dunk their stale buns. Kurt eyed Mark Shaw beadily.

'Had a good night?'

'Sure.' The young fellow smiled over to Charity as she filled a tin mug with coffee and handed it to him.

'We've got to trail those three rats,' gritted Kurt. 'And quit wastin' time. They can't be far off – and—'

'Headin' for Fort Worth, sure as blazes. Are you fit enough, my friend?'

'Fit enough to kill them three single-handed. You can ride on, mister. *Adios*!'

'Why the border lingo?' The other smiled infuriatingly again. 'I figure to go with Charity.'

'Ain't you got other things to do?'

Martin Shaw nodded thoughtfully and brought out the small carving of the totem pole. Balancing it in his hand, he examined the miniature carefully. Kurt stared.

'Yuh seem to value that bit of wood?'

'My brother died because of it.'

'Yeah. But does that make it worth anything?'

'Could be. It's a marker. The Indians use these things as mementoes of their family affairs – markers to ancestral graves – and treasure.'

'Yeah. I know something about them. But your brother weren't no Injun, Mr Shaw.'

'He was as white as me,' snapped Mark Shaw. 'But he had real friends among the red men.'

'Yeah? Care to tell me more?'

'He lived with a squaw, damn yuh – and she gave him this marker.'

'All right – but what the hell's the use of it?'

'There's a clue to a family treasure on the markings on this little totem stick,' snapped the other. 'An' that's all I'm gonna tell you. My brother was killed – and like you I want to find the rat who did it – but you are after Billy's killers – but there ain't no connection. You stick to your feud an' I'll stick to mine.'

'You want the man who killed your brother, huh?' Kurt stared quietly at the other man and for a moment animosity faded.

'Yuh got it in one.'

Pretty soon they were ready to ride out, a party of four, and as they went through the semi-desert in the direction of Fort Worth, following a trail through some buttes and a lot of mesquite, they saw the ruts and hoof-marks, horse droppings and old camp-fires that denoted clearly that this was a main route into the growing town. Kurt and the girls frequently topped low hills to take a look for miles around, but they saw no sign of the three killers they wanted. It seemed the men were wasting little time in getting straight to Fort Worth, which figured for men who wanted to use gold to buy some of the comforts of frontier life.

Fort Worth had grown over the years, Kurt realized, remembering he had not been to the town for a long time and that the population was obviously growing every day. Built on the Trinity River and named after the worthy who had founded the place as one of a chain of forts to protect the border settlements, a General W.J. Worth, it was now a thriving trading centre and recently, in 1875, had been incorporated as a city. The Texas and Pacific Railroad had just reached the place, where stockyards held cattle for shipping. The Indian population had been driven out over the years and men

and women of every European ancenstry were filling
the place, building shacks and erecting tents, with
honest traders rubbing shoulders with the dregs of the
West, of all sexes. Gold and Colt firearms were the
common currency.

Kurt reined in the horses as they paused on a rise to
survey the scene. They could see the railtracks, the
shanties, the false-fronted saloons, the stockyards,
especially these, because they could smell the cattle.

'Big!' commented Kurt. 'Makes Cragside look like a
tin-pot place.'

'We ain't sightseein',' snapped Rose, her hair blowing in the persistent breeze that always came down
from the distant hills.

'We want to kill three men,' added Charity in a
quiet, almost tired, tone. 'Ain't it going to be hell findin'
them here?'

'They'll be spending,' said Kurt. 'They'll have dollars
in their pockets faster than you can weigh out gold in
an assayer's office.'

'You figure to look in the saloons first thing?' asked
Mark Shaw.

'I can do that alone. I still got a good trigger finger.'

As he sat his tall horse, the fine Big Feller, Kurt
looked confident and fit. He had taken his arm out of
the sling but he had a padded bandage under his shirt
in case the wound bled again.

'We need grub,' said Charity. 'And a soak in a big hot
tub of soapy water. I'm not sure – but I think you
fellers like to smell of horse and sweat.'

'Maybe I can scrub your back?' Mark Shaw jigged
his horse around to the nearby tie rail outside a saloon.

The girls parted from the two men and headed for a
big estabishment that advertised: HOT BATHS – TEN

CENTS. – TOE-NAILS CLIPPED. SOAP FREE.

'Ten cents!' exclaimed Kurt. 'Now ain't that inflation?'

The two men went into the saloon, content to take their sweat and dust with them. The sight of foaming tankards of ale drove almost everything out of their minds.

But not everything. Kurt was scanning all the customers in the saloon right from the start. He had a picture of three villains, one a 'breed, one a young desperado with a shock of hair and maybe a wounded arm, and the third a lean grim bastard.

There were plenty in the rough saloon to fill that bill, but no young man with an arm tied in a sling. And half-breed gents seemed scarce although he noticed two full-blood Indians who had their backs in a corner while they cautiously watched everyone else. Kurt thought Fort Worth – or at least this saloon – must be a tolerant place because in many towns the Indian population were often not welcome in drinking dens. He swung his gaze again and fingered his beard. He wanted to feel clean-shaven again, not that a smooth chin was always a common urge among Western men. And he figured his hair needed a trim.

'Maybe the girls have finished their bath?'

'Maybe not. You ought to know the ladies like to take a lot of time over things like that.' Mark Shaw grinned.

Kurt stared him out.

'What the hell d'you know about ladies?' he growled. It was a stupid question because the Western man was a big galoot.

Kurt put his mug down. 'Let's git goin'.'

They were round at the bath house a few minutes later and were able to see through a bead curtain that

Charity and Rose were still up to their necks in warm soapy water.

A negro lady waddled up. 'You can't stick around here. This is for ladies. Shame on youse two gents.'

'All right,' gritted Kurt. 'Let's git rid of our trail shit. Then we take a look-see around this gawdforsaken overgrown cow-town!'

In another section of the bath house they were soon in tubs of water, their clothes hooked up with the guns behind a partition. As they rubbed the red carbolic soap over their private parts and then splashed the steamy water over their heads, they stared at each other.

Mark Shaw grinned at Kurt. 'Say, you still mad at me?'

'You nicked my gal.'

'She ain't your gal. She's Charity Brendan, a lady with a mind of her own. Anyway, yuh ought to be ashamed of yourself, Kurt Kallon, screwing two gals who are pals.'

'Why you – you . . . .'

Kurt reached over, got out of his tub and stood naked as a Nubian statue and swung a punch at the other man. Quick to retaliate, Mark Shaw leaped from his vat of soapy water and faced up to Kurt, his fists raised in the time-honoured stance of the prize-fighter. Both men swung punches at each other and jarred knuckles into jaws. Then they circled again, eyes gleaming in antagonism, flesh wet and soapy, their bodies stark naked.

'You ain't decent!' roared Mark Shaw. 'I mean – two gals – hell, I wouldn't behave like that.'

'Depends on the gals, don't it!' yelled Kurt Kallon 'Aw, balls – you are one annoyin' bucko!' Again he swung a punch at the other man and connected good and solid with Mark Shaw's nose. Blood streamed at once and then thinned amongst the water on Mark's body. Quick as Kurt, he rammed a one-two at the taller man and got satisfaction when Kurt's head jerked back. Tears clouded Kurt's vision, but they were not tears of sorrow. A minute later, after some weaving of muscular arms, they waded back into each other's bodies. A man tried to intervene but got pushed around for his pains and he retreated, yelling for some other man to stop the fight.

The man who finally pushed between Kurt and Mark was a bulky male who had once been a wrestler but now, at the age of sixty, had a paunch that wasn't to his advantage. But he had weight and two young fighting men did not scare him. He reached out.

With two capable hands he was able to reach two men and the part of their bodies he chose to grip and squeeze were certainly not in the Marquis of Queensberry rule-book! He grabbed and pulled at the very private flesh! Two young bucko fools suddenly howled their outrage. They buckled and tried to escape. The huge man held them for another two minutes and then smiled a wide fat smile.

'Guess that'll stop yuh. You two are chasin' off my customers. Yuh wanna fight – git to hell outa here!'

The noise attracted two men from another part of the building, who were respectably clothed, and two girls who were now neatly clad in blue jean material and blouses. The girls stared. Both had wet hair. Both looked as beautiful as an artist's portrait, one gently blonde and the other with glowing red hair. They stared and laughed at the naked men. Rose, of course, was really concerned at the sight of Kurt's wound which was now opened up again and bleeding.

'Cain't leave 'em for five minutes,' shrilled Charity.

'Get some clothes on!' snapped Rose. 'And that wound will need bandaging again, you crazy man!'

With tempers subsiding as quickly as they had arisen, Kurt and Mark Shaw got back into their range gear, buckled on belts and pulled dusty hats down over unruly damp hair.

'We've got to eat,' snapped Kurt. 'And then start some serious searching for our three bastard killers.'

They were all in a better mood after they'd consumed some good steak and mustard, mashed spuds and beans. At the table, Charity leaned forward and asked: 'Do you hate those three swines? Aren't we in danger of losing sight of what they have done? Oh, I know Billy was our sidekick but this trail seems to be losing purpose.'

'Not with me,' lipped Rose.

'I hate 'em,' snapped Kurt. 'An' they got the gold.'

'Gold, huh,' reflected Mark Shaw. 'Now who the hell does that gold belong to?'

'Not me,' snapped Kurt. 'I said I'd lodge it with the marshal in this town, all legal like. Damned if I'll allow those three snakeroos to spend it.'

'I bet they're doin' just that right now. Now where do we look for three louses with gold to spend?'

TEN

'Look in at Joy's Palace,' suggested Jake Duerr and he leaned back in his seat. His desk was big and carved and all around him on the walls of the large office were Wanted posters of the West's current crop of villains, robbers and murderers. Rifles were stacked in a rich mahogany case and there was an Indian rug on the floor. Jake Duerr was as big as his job in life, Town Marshal of Fort Worth, with a couple of other officers to call to hand when things got rough.

'Why Joy's Palace?' asked Kurt. He and the two girls had crowded into the office while Mark Shaw stood at the door viewing the passing scene: the horses, the riders, the wagons and folks on the boardwalks.

'Joy loves gold,' said Jake Duerr. 'She runs that brothel like a saloon and assayer's office rolled into one. She figures gold is better than dollars because she can cheat the fool miners better.'

'Brothel, huh?' Kurt looked at Rose. 'These two gals don't know nothin' about such things, Marshal, an' I don't think they want to hear such talk. Where is this damned Joy's Palace?'

'Right on the corner of Main Street. You can't miss it. But let me tell you, mister, I don't let galoots take the law into their own hands. Fort Worth is a fine town. And I jail any man shootin' off for no reason an' me and Judge Tarrant hang murderers just about every month. Got it? You bunch watch your step.' The marshal looked doubtfully at the Colt hardware slung around the shapely waists of the two girls. 'I ain't seen many gun-totin' females for some time – not with Colts as big as their tits!'

And then they were out in the street, where the sun threw heat over the town and the distant terrain. 'It's a lead,' said Kurt. 'We got to start somewhere.'

'Big cheeky swine!' muttered Charity. 'Big tits indeed!'

'I think he was looking at you, darling!' said Rose sweetly.

They had left the animals in a livery where they'd get a much-needed rub down and plenty of feed. So they went into their cowboy gait; like all riders who spent too much time astride a horse's rib-cage. And then after ten minutes' amble they stared up at the large ornate false-front of Joy's Palace. The sun told them it was just past midday and the evidence was that the Palace had a steady stream of visitors, and they were nearly all men.

'I should ha' known.' Kurt stared at the batwings and the draped windows on the first floor. 'This place is not for you two gals.'

A fat floosie in a green taffeta dress reaching to her ankles, but very revealing at the bodice, waddled through the batwings and stared insolently at Kurt and Mark, her mouth daubed with some red polish. She flicked a glance at the two girls.

'Hey? You want work? Are they lookin' for a job, fellers?'

'We want to buy gold.'

'See Joy. She handles that. Me – I jest deal with dames.'

Mark Shaw tapped Kurt's arm. 'We ain't buyin' gold – but we could be buyin' grief. See them galoots?'

They were inside the darkish interior of the place, and the two girls had gone off to look at a ladies' drapery emporium on the other side of the main stem. Mark pointed discreetly at two menacing figures who stood just inside the main passage, hefty Colts prominent on tight gun-belts. Both hands had gunny stamped all over their taut faces. They wore red shirts tucked into brown cord pants, all of which was new and spotless, and they kept new Stetsons firmly on blond hair that grew thickly down the back of their necks. Both men cast Kurt and Mark a searching glare from young hard eyes.

'You want wimmen or a drink?' one gunny lipped.

'Drinks, pal.' Mark Shaw threw the answer with equal directness.

The men waved at the interior.

The extravagantly-furnished bar-lounge had an odour thick with the presence of cheap women more than the smell of drink. The females were just about everywhere, sitting at tables with men, some perched on hard male knees and others simply standing at the mahogany bar. The shelves in front of the long bar-mirrors were stacked with bottles of every drink possible to find in a cow-town. Some of the more exotic wines had arrived by rail from sources a long way from Texas.

A door marked ASSAYER'S OFFICE looked very solid and private, set in a corner of the lounge bar, and the two men decided this was where business in gold was done. Just to clinch things, Kurt asked the bartender with the handlebar moustache:

'Where can we find Joy?'

'You mean the boss – or are yuh talkin' about pleasure?' chuckled the man.

'The boss.'

'Knock on the assayer's door but don't walk in until you get a reply.'

Kurt and Mark slowly placed the mugs of warm beer down on the counter, walked over and knocked. A voice which sounded like a man's throaty answer yelled: 'Yeah? In!'

So Kurt turned the handle carefully and walked in with Mark. They found themselves staring at a big .45 held in a large fist by a lady who sat in a huge horsehair armchair. She was voluminously clothed in a red dress which could have draped a big window. She had brazen blonde hair which tumbled around her mannish face in large curls and made her appear positively ugly. This female, Kurt and Mark realized, was Joy. She couldn't be anyone else.

'What do you gents want?' The gun pointed at their guts. The black eyes in the leathery female face showed no softness or cordiality. 'It's business only in here.'

'Yeah, gold business,' Kurt said. 'We know. Gold is our business.'

'You're in the right joint. Buyin' or sellin'?'

Mark looked cautiously at Kurt and then at the ugly chunk of fashioned metal which was the .45 and then at Joy's equally ugly features. Right behind the lady was a huge safe set on massive wooden posts; Kurt could read the legend: H. WALDORF. MICHIGAN. Thr brass plate was highly polished. The safe was impregnable.

Joy noticed their eyes on the safe.

'There's no way you could open it even if you came in the middle of the night with dynamite. And there's always a guard on hand. Now what is it with you two boys?'

'Have you had three gents in here sellin' gold dust and nuggets – one *hombre* a 'breed, one a young bucko with long hair and the third feller an embittered lean snakeroo?'

For a long time Joy's face looked grim. 'You figure I'm an information service?'

'You're a lady,' stated Mark Shaw with a smile on his good-looking face. And then with an effrontery that amazed Kurt and even took the lady by surprise, he leaned close to her, ignoring the gun, and kissed her on the lips with beautiful delicacy. The gentlemanly touch of mouths was so tender and prolonged that Joy did not move or flinch. When Mark Shaw eased back, still smiling – even looking as if he had enjoyed the meeting of lips – the leathery lady stared at him for a long time, unblinking, impassive as if she was carved out of granite, the gun seemingly frozen in her hand. Then slowly she smiled, which was a grotesque curve of her mouth. Her old eyes softened and for a minute which seemed to Kurt to be an eternity, she looked amazingly feminine, her reddened gash of a mouth almost soft with some strangely womanly pleasure.

She held Mark Shaw's gleaming eyes. She stared at his lips as if inviting another kiss.

Then she croaked: 'You're a lovely young feller. I ain't been kissed like that for a helluva long time. I don't believe it! You kinda enjoyed kissing my ugly mug, didn't ya?'

'You are a lovely lady, Joy,' breathed Mark Shaw and

the conviction in his gentle tones made Kurt Kallon marvel.

'I'm an old hag!'

'That ain't so. You remind me of my dear old ma. She was a hard lady but beautiful with it – like you are, Joy. I knew it the moment I saw yuh. Joy, you're all lovely lady!'

Kurt Kallon barely believed the change in the woman, from an ugly bitch to a softly feminine person whose eyes and mouth seemed to tremble into a mould that was definitely womanly. The gun lowered. She smiled, again a crooked twist, but a smile nevertheless. Kurt thought maybe it was the first time she had smiled in years.

'You're like a young feller I knew – aw – years ago – an' he said I was lovely. Yeah, he figured I was lovely. Jeeze, that was a hundred years ago, wasn't it? Aw! Shit! What do you two boys really want?'

'Just tell us about the three ginks we mentioned.' Mark Shaw treated the lady to another handsome smile and she soaked it up with a pleasure that was almost pathetic. 'They did sell you gold, didn't they, Joy, darlin' lady?'

Kurt maintained his fixed smile with an effort and watched the big fat lady soften into a pliant mould.

'Yeah,' she said eagerly. 'Three ginks, like yuh said, lovely boy. I didn't like 'em. But it was business. Yeah, I bought the gold. They said they'd be back with more.'

'More?' Kurt's snapped query almost broke the spell. She flicked him a glance with eyes that seemed to harden for a brief second and then soften when she turned her head again to Mark Shaw and his pleading smiles.

'Yup. They said they had more gold. So I told them

to come in any time. Not that I trust them. I've told my two gunnies to come round to the back curtain iffen they knock on my door.'

Kurt figured it was time to get out while the magic spell that Mark Shaw had created within the woman lasted.

With a prosaic scraping of boots on the wood floor as they made an exit, they reached the boardwalk outside. Kurt turned to Mark.

'Get that damned fool expression off your mug! Gawd, you amazed me. Here's Charity an' Rose. Hell, how did yuh do it? I'd better not tell Charity you got all that damned sexy style!'

The two girls were walking across the main stem to meet them. Then Mark Shaw said: 'The killers are coming back to see Joy.'

Kurt nodded. 'Yeah! Kinda strange, huh? They ain't got no more gold.'

'Exactly. So what's the trick?'

'Yeah, must be a scheme.'

'They're robbin' hell-bents, ain't they?'

'No doubt about that. And killers. Yeah, they got the scent of gold in their lousy brains. But, Mark, they'd be walkin' into guns if they attempted anythin' like that – and how would they open that damned giant of a safe?'

Mark Shaw had time to mutter: 'That's a good question.' Then his arms were full of an exuberant Charity Brendan. Kurt, too, found a scented woman. Rose had decided she wanted Kurt Kallon.

When the delights of kissing Rose had faded to a decent level, and the old ladies on the boardwalk had tut-tutted and passed on, Kurt and Mark got around to discussing the three killers in a sane manner. They went into a little eating-house.

'Now what's all this about those three killers?' Rose leaned forward. 'Let's go over the facts.'

'If they are returning to Joy's Palace,' mused Kurt, 'it's because they've got the mad notion they can rob the lady of her gold – and she must have a fortune in that tough old safe.'

'They could end up real dead.' Rose touched Kurt's arm. 'That would save you from having to kill them.'

'I'm goin' to kill them. Billy is still a real memory.'

'My lovely pard will always be a real memory to me, too,' said Rose. 'But what happens to me if you end up a cadaver on account of them three skunks?'

There was no answer to that. The four went out on to the boardwalk and found a long wood-plank seat in the afternoon sun. They sat and watched the passing scene, the never-ending trail of riders of all types, from Mex saddle-bums to prosperous ranchers out to meet bankers and business partners. The street was full of wheeled traffic; the stage was disembarking some local travellers from points other than those served by the railroad. High up the valley, the Trinity River flowed and served as a passage for men who came down from the placer mines to visit town and bring their gold with them.

Kurt examined his gun with the hard realization within him that maybe he would at long last get the chance to blast the three killers. Mark Shaw sat stern-faced, a marked contrast to his smiling act with Joy at her Palace.

Then as they sat in the alcove on the boardwalk, almost hidden by weird cactus plants in large tubs, the three hardcases they sought came slowly riding down the street and hitched their horses with slow deliberation to the tie rail outside Joy's Palace.

Kurt sat tensed, watching almost in disbelief the way the three acted. The Kid Curtis galoot had discarded his sling, although he held his arm limply by his side. They were bearded, careless about their appearance, with trail dust almost a disguise. The 'breed was a man with a mask for a face. Hec Redman looked positively menacing in every taut muscle of his body.

And then the men dismounted, purposely, without a word.

ELEVEN

'Let's git in there an' heist that gold!' Hec Redman spat a stream of tobacco juice to the dirt road. Chewing on a wad was a habit he returned to every so often, when money was to hand to buy a quid. 'We're gonna be millionaires.'

'I figure dynamite is the best way,' slurred Kid Curtis. 'At night, Hec, when that old hag is asleep.'

'She's got guards!' hissed the other.

Harry stared at the ornate façade of Joy's Palace. 'Dynamite makes a hell of a row. I figure Hec's trick will be the best.'

Hec's bearded face twisted in a sardonic smile. 'You got it right, Harry. We got guns – that's all we need. Hell, we did something like this way back in Pawnee City, remember?'

Hidden behind the large tubs that contained the spiky-leaved cactus plants, Kurt and the other three watched and studied the slow movements of the three rogues. The men were oddly deliberate, as if a snail's pace was the best preliminary to ultimate action. It seemed that even dangerous men needed moments in which to hype up their motives.

'Should we go after them now?' Mark Shaw at this moment deferred to Kurt.

135

Rose touched Kurt's arm. 'Dear God, maybe they'll end up dead without you having to contest them.'

Charity glanced at her friend and nodded, a little fear stirring in her heart. She came close to Mark. She held his sleeve as if to detain him, but she knew there was no retreat for the two men.

'Give this damned play another minute. We'll follow those three rats into the Palace. Rose might be right. They could end up dead without us firing a shot.'

'Somehow I don't think you'll enjoy that,' muttered Mark Shaw.

Kurt nodded as he watched the three hell-bents move through the batwings in to Joy's Palace. He even saw the two gunhands stationed there nod to the men as if they recognized them as customers. Then it seemed it was time for action.

Kurt fisted Mark's shoulder. 'Let's go. You two gals just stick around.'

'Maybe you'd enjoy some more tea,' suggested Mark. He got a fierce glance for his attempt at a joke.

Kurt Kallon knew they were playing this whole scenario by ear and anything could happen where men and guns were concerned. The rogues were doing the same crazy thing, banking on good luck, banking that events would go their way and in the worst solution guns and death would solve everything. He thought it was unbelievable that Hec Redman could even hope to open the massive safe without explosives or keys, and surely Joy or some trusty held them. Just what did Hec Redman figure to do?

Maybe Joy was taking time off from her bar stint in her stronghold office. She was a big woman with an appetite for most things. Maybe she was eating, or having a nap, or maybe just brushing her long garish

curls? She could be anywhere. Did Hec Redman figure
to draw and out-gun her many guards? Had Hec
Redman, the villain, just gone crazy, figuring he just
had to barge in?

In actual fact Hec and his two partners had information that Kurt did not possess. When they had sold
the woman the stolen gold they had learnt that Joy
was a lady of regular habits. She spent one hour off
and one hour on meeting miners with gold to sell or
anyone else who wanted to deal in gold.

The hellions knew Joy would be at her desk right at
that moment.

The guards watched the progress of the three dirty
roughnecks and, having seen them earlier, figured they
wished to do business with their boss, the lady of the
House, and House it was apart from gold, where hard
males sought pleasure when they weren't making prof-
its.

As the entrance was part of the saloon, there were a
number of customers in every frontier type of garb, and
when Kurt and Mark strode in they were not unusual.
Kurt stared around with fast glances.

'They've disappeared!' He snapped the remark to
the young fellow at his side. Mark Shaw nodded.

'They've gone straight to see Joy, I guess.'

'Well, they ain't got gold to sell. They've got robbery
in mind. How the blazes do they figure to open that
safe? And how are they goin' to get away with it with
gunny guards at Joy's beck an' call?'

Kurt reckoned the answers had to be behind that
solid mahogany door, so they brushed past the drinking clients and walked quickly up to the office. They
did not know what to expect. They did not intend to
give the customary knock and wait for Joy to answer.

Kurt went in fast, with Mark Shaw at his heel. Kurt's 44-40 Peacemaker was like a small howitzer in his fist. The door swung in. Kurt and Mark pushed into the office. One swift glance was enough. Joy was not sitting in her horsehair chair and she was not pointing a gun.

Grimly, it was action time. The three killers they sought had the hefty lady flat on the Indian carpet and were standing over her. In an unusual twist to their preferred method of dealing with enemies, the three cruel men were holding knives to Joy's face and to her body. It seemed that Hec Redman realized that a knife was a silent way of dealing with opposition.

'Open that damned safe, you ugly bitch – or we carve your mug into bloody ribbons!' Hec Redman knew just how to make a threat real.

'Go to hell!' screamed Joy.

The whole stark situation was one where men on sudden impulse could dive into any kind of violent reaction. Kurt and his new sidekick, Mark, just flung themselves at the three range bastards, fists naturally flying out in sheer rage. They were men in a fury and the guns to hand were momentarily forgotten! Fists were always a man's natural weapons and strange as it might seem, sticks and stones – and guns – came second. Kurt and Mark flung at the other range cusses, ramming out rock-hard fists in instant rage.

It was hatred of a sort. They were men who just naturally hated the others. Joy, on the floor, screamed again, the noise totally dampened by the thick walls and the solid door to her office. Kurt and Mark simply wanted instant revenge on the three hellions who had caused so much trouble, including death. A physical collision was the instinctive way, with men hurling their bodies at the enemy. Primitive hate boiled up.

Kid Curtis felt fear jag through him and he dropped his knife. He had been enjoying the savage satisfaction of threatening to carve up the woman. They had wrenched at her bodice and her ample flesh was exposed and ready for the first cut. The sight of Kurt and the other man jolted a scare through him. He instinctively tried to grab at his Colt.

Kurt hefted the gun from his fist even as it appeared in sight. Then a punch landed on the young ruffian's jaw, making him lurch back against the wall.

Hec Redman slashed with his knife at Mark Shaw, eyes blazing with pure hate. He'd figured they were within seconds of forcing the old bitch to open the safe containing a fortune in gold, a millionaire's unlimited wealth, a kind of Aladdin's cave of gold, and now it was all at risk.

The wicked knife sliced through thin air because Mark Shaw had reactions as swift as those of Kurt Kallon. The blade hacked inches away from Mark's face.

Harry was thrown into the fight, his usual caution driven away by his own particular brand of anger. He was the only one to draw a gun but the weapon never exploded because Kurt whipped around to face the danger, his fists ramming with terrible fury at the part-Indian. Harry did not like fists. True, he could endure pain stoically, some part of his heritage giving him this quality, but hard fists on the end of swinging arms he could not take. His gun was rammed out of his grip and thudded to the carpeted floor.

Kurt had pounded bunched fists into the face of Kid Curtis, feeling some agony streak through his shoulder wound again, but that did not matter, and the young thug was on the floor. So Kurt gave Harry's thin sallow face the pounding the man had invited. Harry sagged to the floor, his nose pouring blood and his dusty range shirt suddenly sticky with the mess.

Mark Shaw gripped Hec Redman's knife-wrist, struggling to stop the blade from slashing again at his face. The man was possessed with some super-strength, strange in a thin frame in poor condition because of bad nourishment, but seemingly Hec Redman was burnt up with some rage which was almost volcanic. The lure of gold had got him into this consuming fury, which was something that Mark Shaw had not faced for a long time. He was not by instinct a rough-house fighter. But he dealt with the other man in the natural way, by throwing fists and stopping the thin man in his tracks. Hec Redman sagged, down on his knees, his lousy rage beaten by the physical pain that showed in his face, his nose broken and blood smearing his skin. The man on his knees, roared with pain. Mark did not spare him but slammed mercilessly at the bloodied mask until Hec Redman collapsed, panting, dragging for breath, making sounds like an animal.

It seemed the three men were beaten. Certainly their attempt to steal more gold was thwarted, but there came a crazy play to the scene. Joy scrambled to her feet and tried to throw angry punches at Kid Curtis. He pushed her to one side, then dived for a Colt gun lying on the floor. He gripped it in brief seconds, then whirled round to Joy, his young body moving with feline litheness. He rammed the gun into her side, backing round, holding her with one arm that was strengthened by rage.

'Back off – all of yuh! I'll kill her, by hell!'

All the men froze in seconds, as though in a tableau,

wariness and disbelief flooding tensed bodies, even those of the three villains.

Hec Redman lurched to his feet, clutching at this one chance, and Harry recovered from punishment, swaying, hissing his ugly threats.

'Let's get out!' Hec Redman knew the crazy scene was too grotesque to be sustainable, with guards by the dozen in the building and ready to crash in if the sound of one shot was heard.

The three villains regrouped, crowding around Kid Curtis and the fat old proprietor of Joy's Palace, pushing her to the door, gun viciously rammed into her ample flesh. Just one uncontrolled squeeze on the trigger and all hell would be let loose in that building. And of course, Joy would die.

Kurt had no real regard for the old avaricious female but she was a human being and entitled to live her own life. Some higher fate would punish her ultimately.

Kurt just nodded to Mark Shaw, who took the warning and stood still while the killer men backed, holding the woman as hostage. Could he chance a shot? Kurt thought furiously. If he triggered, the woman would be as good as dead – even if a dirty villain got his come-uppance. Kallon's gun loomed, a lethal chunk of weaponry, heavy in his fist, but restrained action by the thought that the woman might die if guns exploded and slugs spat out.

Three angry vicious men were snarling slurred comments.

'Let's git out!'

And: 'Don't fire, Kid! This joint is full of gun-hands.'

And: 'Git to horses, Hec – just git outa this!'

The irksome sight of the three crowding the doorway with the fat lady of the establishment filled Kurt's gut with anger, but the scene held. If he fired, Kid Curtis would finger his own trigger and in a second there would be mayhem. Kurt Kallon cursed inwardly, using some choice words he had never hauled out of the cesspool for a long time.

Even the three hard men needed to act swiftly, probably praying in their own evil way for hells own luck. They got it.

Hec Redman heaved the door open and Kid Curtis pushed Joy out into the bar lounge, opposite some tables where men sat hefting cards and drinking from big tankards. Seeing guns poking threats, the drinking men froze.

Even the gunny guards near the batwings were cowed into hesitation, red-blooded rannigans though they were. They had to hang back while the three desperate killer-men made their crazy way to the boardwalk outside, taking the screaming Joy with them.

They came out on to the street, stamping their riding boots on the boardwalk. Kurt and Mark Shaw followed, feeling useless because the life of the fat lady hung in the balance. One searing shot from a Colt and everything could change.

Then the whole scenario changed.

As the group of desperadoes stamped out on to the boardwalk, looking for horses to enable them to make a getaway, Charity and Rose appeared from nowhere. In the blink of an eye, they stood in the way of the three killers they so desperately wanted to eliminate. And then Hec Redman, his vicious blood galvanized by anger, grabbed at the blonde Charity, hefted her Colt from her holster with real speed. He gripped Charity with stringy strength in his arms and shoved the gun in her side.

'Git!' He pushed her to the horses at the tie rail. Kid Curtis saw the trick, knowing what Redman meant to do. He hurled the fat lady to one side on the boardwalk, sending her sprawling. As she tumbled she howled her fright and rage.

Kurt cursed again; his Peacemaker for now was just a chunk of metal, it seemed. Hec Redman rammed Charity to the back of his horse. The creature bucked in fright, kicking out, causing confusion among the other animals that were hitched there.

And then, in crazy confusion, the three desperate hell-bent men were hurling themselves with practised speed into saddle leather, Charity was heaved in front of Hec Redman, then the animals pranced in startled fear and leaped off.

Kurt Kallon shot at Hec Redman, a risky slug because the hot metal might have bitten into flesh just about anywhere, maybe even the body of the young blonde girl he loved as much as he loved Rose.

His slug spat venomously through the thin evening air and missed the stringy villain. Mark Shaw tried a fast bullet, aiming at Harry, the vile, furtive 'breed. The horses bucked and raced ahead, leaving the frontage of Joy's Palace far behind. Mark's slug tore the air and nothing else.

Then guns were booming in all directions as the guards whom Joy hired for protection really got into the act and loosed off hot lead. Incredibly, as it sometimes happened in the mêlées, the bullets missed human targets because of the bucking, racing animals, then Hec Redman and his reckless sidekicks were tearing down the main stem of Fort Worth, scattering other riders, nearly colliding with wagons and a coach. They were riding to hell and freedom, it seemed. Charity was held in a vicious grip by the desperate renegade, Hec Redman. She struggled and screamed, but he held her. The horse plunged dangerously down the main street, rounded a bend and then was gone, with Kid Curtis and Harry hard-riding alongside. Kurt cursed in impotent frustration.

His horse – and the others – were stabled!

TWELVE

Sure as they were men with red blood, they scorched around to the livery, Rose with them, not to be left behind. Fear for Charity lent her wings. The three pushed and shoved into the stables, flinging yelled, incoherent comments to the elderly hostler; then in frantic seconds, it seemed, they were mounted, in spite of the time it took to throw leather on to the animals' backs.

The main stem was clear of the three furiously riding villains and not even a trail of dust showed where they had gone. But Kurt Kallon had a good idea of the direction these men would take.

'The hills! Sure as hell – past the Trinity River – to the hills!'

Fort Worth was a town bordered by the river and in the lee of the distant hills, a locale where the placer miners had their claims in the stream. The waters came down from the Yellow Hills in a torrent during the winter months and then dried up to a trickle during the hot weeks of the summer. The ranchers on the spreads leading to the hills had ample water in the rainy season, with boreholes and windmills to supply moisture for the cattle, or they could drive the beeves

145

down to the nearest bend in the river where they could drink their fill, and where the grass was greener.

Kurt and Mark thrashed their mounts ever onward; Rose keeping up with difficulty on her less powerful animal. Then, when they had crested a shale rise they stopped and stared around for sight of the vicious rogues.

They were nowhere in sight. There was not even a tell-tale cloud of dust to be seen. The worn trail stretched ahead, with hoof-marks aplenty, but apparently they were old trail-signs, made long ago by the miners heading out of town with their supplies for a long spell in the Yellow Hills.

'Where in tarnation are they?' Kurt sat tall in the saddle and stared all around, taking in the semi-desert land where the cactus was spreading among the defiles and gullies. Some jagged buttes rose out of the arid land a few miles ahead, and there was an eerie silence everywhere.

'Not even a hoof-beat,' snapped Kurt.

'Try the old Injun trick,' suggested Mark. He slid from his saddle, placed his ear to the earth and listened intently for some minutes. Then he slowly got up, took off his hat and mopped his brow.

'Not a sound. They've gone to ground – somewhere.'

'Yeah – somewhere.' grated Kurt. He stared at the distant buttes. The tall spires of sandstone were eroded by centuries of wind and winter rains and looked like gargoyles. Home for rattlers he figured, and providing perches for buzzards. 'Them damned buttes! Can't be anywhere else! One of their nags has a double load, remember.'

'I ain't goin' to forget that,' Mark rapped back.

Kurt exchanged glances with him. 'You an' Charity – is it for real? I mean, what the hell are your intentions, mister?'

'Same as yours towards Rose.'

'I aim to git a preacher when we get all this durned business settled with them killer scumbitches.'

'Same with me.' Mark gave a thin smile. 'Yuh sure as hell can't marry them both, Kurt.'

'Yeah. Seems like I got to make up my mind.'

The horses slowly eased down from the shale slope, the rattle of hooves dislodging rock the only sound for miles around. A slight breeze came down steadily from the Yellow Hills, suggesting life and movement in the area, as if it was the only presence in the arid quiet land. But Kurt knew for sure the three cursed hellions were out there somewhere, as dangerous as the rattlers, but predators of the worst kind, men who killed for pleasure and greed.

Rose had heard the exchange of remarks and with a smile on her red lips she rode her animal close to Kurt.

'Do you mean that – about a preacher – Kurt?'

He reached across. His mouth hunted for her lips and he gave her an unashamedly long kiss and then pushed her back with a smile.

'C'mon! We got to find Charity. Now just what in hell do they aim to do with her? I mean, why kidnap her like this?'

'Well, she ain't got no gold!' Mark Shaw rowelled his horse. 'If they harm Charity, I'll kill the three of 'em with my bare hands!'

Kurt nodded and raced his horse into a full lope, heading with the others for the jagged yellow sandstone buttes. The gold that the old-timers had so greedily acquired was gone. Scattered, belonged now to others. Kurt could not control that now. It seemed that Snap and Dad Bowker had died in vain, like a lot more before them where gold was concerned. And yet it went on, this quest for wealth. And Mark Shaw had his strange miniature totem pole. What were the mysteries associated with this odd length of Indian marker? Where would it take him?

Kurt steadily guided his horse to the distant yellow buttes feeling that somehow there might be final answers among their dusky shadows. Charity had to be rescued. The awful alternative for her was a violent death.

Three surly enraged men, tired of riding, hungry and parched through lack of water, flung themselves from the blowing horses and lay flat on the sandy cave-like cleft in the largest of the yellow buttes. They glared around, needing rest, somewhere to pause and consider their plans, or lack of them. Charity had been propelled to a rocky crevice, her panting horse trailing leathers to one side.

She glared defiance at the three bitter hardcases. 'They'll kill yuh! Yuh can't win!'

'Shut your damned yap!' Hec Redman strode over in a rage and kicked at the girl. She felt tears spring to her eyes. But through this haze of moisture, she eyed the man furiously.

'I'll kill you myself – if I get the chance.'

'You ain't got a hogleg!' snarled Kid Curtis. Dirty bad temper filled his wicked young heart, the pain in his wound adding to his nastiness.

'What do we want with this squaw?' Harry walked over and stared at the girl, his black eyes glinting. 'She ain't no use.'

'She might be,' said Hec Redman. 'We ain't out o' this mess as yet.'

He stared evilly, eyeing her, his gaze travelling over her womanly shape until she felt as if cockroaches were crawling over her flesh.

'She's a damned nuisance,' snapped Harry.

'She's a hostage, ain't she?' hissed the tall thin range rat. 'Who knows? We might be able to use her.'

'Better dead.' Harry's vulpine features looked at Charity as if he would enjoy inflicting pain on to a white woman with this particular type of corn-coloured blonde hair. Although the sun had tanned her face, she was still the typical pretty blonde woman and so utterly different from Harry with his dark visage and black eyes. He just hated her for that reason.

'We keep her alive,' gritted Hec Redman. 'Those two bastards will be on our trail.'

'We still got *dinero* from this gold sale,' commented Kid Curtis. 'An' iffen the horses git some rest we could be on our way.'

'That's for sure,' sneered Hec Redman. 'You figure I wanna stick around this goddamned dry land for ever?'

The Trinity River was some miles distant and the garish yellow soils around the jagged buttes gave little promise of drinkable water. Hec had realized that their water bottles were a bit low. He moved restlessly around the cave-like opening, stopped and stared out across the empty land.

'Them stinkin' interfering fellers will be on to us pretty soon.'

'They might not find us,' snapped Kid Curtis.

'Aw, be your age! Where in hell d'yuh git your brains from? Sure they'll locate us. We ought to be goin'.'

'My hoss seems a bit lame.'

Redman pointed viciously at Kid Curtis. 'Reckon yuh should look after the critter a bit better. That nag is between you an' death!'

Kid Curtis sneered at the older man. He sprawled; the pain in his shoulder-wound was making him peevish.

Harry was suddenly curious about the cave-like crevice in the yellow rock. He had been staring at the walls, and he began to perceive drawings scratched in the rock face, some with the semblance of prairie animals of long ago . . . other marks seemed to be the hieroglyphics of an ancient language. Some innate curiosity made him study the old writing. He began to trace the lines with his fingers . . . .

Hec Redman glared at him. 'What's bitin' you?'

'Indian drawings,' said Harry laconically.

'So what?'

'This place was a burial chamber.'

'Ya don't say!' jeered the other. 'So what the hell? I've seen damned Injun drawings afore.'

'This is a bad place.' Harry seemed to flinch away from the rock face. 'Death here. Bad things. Men have died.'

'So what?'

'We might be next.' Harry's comments were typical of him when his thoughts became incoherent and his search for words dried up.

'Damned Injun crap!' yelled Hec Redman. 'Now why the blazes am I stuck with you lot? One wet about the chops – an' the other full of lousy Injun shit.' Harry's black eyes glinted but he seemed lost for further words.

Suddenly Charity sprang up like a tiger, her warm young blood impelling her on. She dived for the opening to the cleft in the butte, her riding boots digging into the sand and shale.

'Hell! We should ha' tied her up!' Hec Redman sprang after her.

Charity did not get very far. The man was a lot older but he had long legs and in the end he dived at her and brought her to the ground just outside the shelter of the cleft. She struggled under him but his arms held her, pushing her soft body into the sand and tufts of grass. He stared into her flushed face, sweating at the sight of her tanned flawless skin and the mass of blonde curls.

'Ain't-cha the beauty? Better than all them poxy bitches in the brothels! Gee, I could take a she-cat like you – an' I will!'

His hands began to pluck at her blouse, tearing at the cotton, an attack which only made Charity fight back with all her strength and furious hands. She clawed at his face – his eyes – struggling and writhing under him. Hec Redman became a madman at this show of resistance and sought to hold her. His way was to hit Charity hard in the face, as he would a man, making her cry with pain, and when she sagged mometarily he pressed down on her, his hands tearing at her shirt again.

Then there came a strange interruption. Harry, who had been fuming with sullen anger at Redman's remarks, grabbed at the other man's arm and hauled him off the girl.

'She ain't for yuh!'

Hec Redman was rammed to the ground by the force of Harry's arms. For some furious seconds he lay there and glared.

'Why, you part Injun crap-head – I'll kill yuh!'

'She's young – not for you!'

'Balls! Outa my way.'

Harry was only using the girl as an excuse to confront Hec Redman; resentment about the way the man had treated him was boiling up. Hec Redman hauled his gun out of the leather and pointed it at the 'breed.

'You're dead!'

'Don't shoot him,' yelled Kid Curtis suddenly. 'Those two bastards are on our trail!'

He had been staring out over the wastelands that lay beyond the buttes. Now he pointed. 'Two riders!'

His cry was enough to stop Hec Redman in his villainous intentions, causing him to swing away and stare into the distance.

'Yeah – them two ornery devils! Hunted us out. You're right, Kid. If I shoot they'll hear the shots.'

'Comin' this way in any case,' commented Kid Curtis angrily. 'I tell yuh – we should ha' kept on riding!'

'Aw, damn them! There's three of us!'

'Yeah? Wal, there's another jasper with them – cruisin' up behind, down the damned trail. Looks like he's on a slow hoss!'

'Who the hell is he?' Hec Redman's sight was not as penetrating as that of Kid Curtis.

'Sure looks like that damned marshal outa Fort Worth! Now why the hell is he ridin' in with them two cusses – and, shit – there's the other gal ridin' with him!'

Hec Redman reached swiftly for his rifle in the

saddle scabbard, slamming his horse further into the cleft in the yellow rock.

'We'll kill the damned lot of 'em! Back up! Git your long smoke-pole, Kid! An' you, too, Harry!'

THIRTEEN

The yellow buttes rose like strange silent sentinels out of the waste of sand and tufted clumps of bunch grass mingled with cholla cactus. The spires of yellow rock had drawn the attention of the party right from the start. Somehow they just knew the three wanted men were hiding there, with Charity as their hostage.

Kurt slowed the headlong pace, Mark Shaw right beside him. The marshal of Fort Worth and Rose had been left somewhere in the rear because of the fast gallop of Big Feller and Mark's mount. But they were only minutes behind and the intentions of the whole party were quite clear. They had to rescue Charity. As to what might happen after that perhaps fate and hot slugs might determine that!

The first shot rang out from the outlandish shapes of the weathered sandstone buttes. Kid Curtis had a foolish idea that the enemy was within range and that he had ammunition to waste. He rapped off three shots with his Colt and then turned viciously to the Winchester he had in his saddle scabbard.

'Yuh wasted that lead!' raged Hec Redman. 'How the hell do yuh expect to hit them at that distance with a hand-gun?'

Kid Curtis made some rude comment about the other's mysterious parentage.

'Crap! I'll git them!'

'That's a damned lawman you're firin' at!'

'He'll hit the dust just the same.'

Hec Redman wondered if the Kid's money was still safely tucked in his belt or his saddle-bag. If Kid Curtis died of lead poisoning, would there be a chance to get his *dinero* and ride the hell out of it?

Kurt and his friends knew that to ride straight up to the others' hiding places in the face of the Colt fire would be taking too many chances. With Rose determined to take part in the hunt for her young pard's killers, they had to be careful. And, anyway, there was no cover out in the wasteland except for a few scattered boulders that had lain for ages in the sand, shale and grass. They just had to stay out of range, realizing the others had rifles.

Jake Duerr rode up, his large body sitting heavily on the blowing nag.

'Holed up, huh? Well, we got 'em to rights.'

'Can we be sure with snakeroos of that type? What about when the sun sinks? Will they make a run for it?'

'We can stake 'em out till then. There's three of us – an' the gal. Even if it is dark, some of us kin stay awake.'

'Those damned killers can do the same.'

The whole set-up changed from a chase to a slow and irksome game of waiting, with the sun slowly assuming the redness of the evening orb and still no sign of movement from the cave-like recesses in the weirdly shaped buttes.

'Resting!' snapped Kurt.

'I figure they'll slink out when it is dark – but

there'll be a moon tonight and we'll get 'em.' Jake Duerr paused. 'I hope you two ain't bent on killin' just for the sake of it. They should stand trial. I only came along with you fellers to see the law obeyed.'

'That might be difficult.' Mark Shaw squatted in the sand beside his horse, the heat of the day still in the earth. That, of course, would soon fade because in this part of Texas the sun sank swiftly as evening turned to night. 'They've got Charity – an' sure as hell I find waitin' hard to accept.'

Kurt compressed his lips and looked at Rose as she stayed close to him, seeking some comfort in his presence.

Back in the cave, where the rock face overhung the cleft, Harry was prowling morosely around the limited confines, staring at the ancient Indian markings while the other two took their ease. Hec Redman finally spat out his tobacco quid because his guts were in turmoil. A hard, vicious man, he suffered from gut trouble, probably because of the hell-bent life he had lived. Kid Curtis felt his aching shoulder and scowled. As for Charity, they had bound her wrists together with some spare manila rope.

Something about the ancient hole in the rock face fascinated Harry; the markings and drawings were beyond his comprehension but all the same this appealed to some strange force in his mind. Indians had drawn these pictures of bison and hunters on horseback; the primitive artists were part of his ancestry. Some affinity with the weird drawings stirred him and he began to mumble in a harsh whisper.

'Will ya shut that crazy row?' Kid Curtis couldn't control his nerves.

Harry turned on him, advanced a step and kicked at

the young man. Kid Curtis leaped up and swung a punch that missed the 'breed. The two of them hefted guns and poked the darkening air between them with the weapons. But they did not let their anger move trigger fingers.

'Cut it out!' snarled Hec Redman. 'We're gonna git out of here! Ain't no flaming use sticking around! We gotta go!'

'Suits me,' boasted Kid Curtis. 'I ain't the type to sit on my arse!'

'Yeah? Well, take note – we move out on the horses nice and easy, no damned row. We might git a head start thataway.'

Hec Redman knew the hope was a desperate one because with determined men out there, including a town marshal, they could be in a fix. But, like all villains, he expected luck to be on his side. So far in a crazy life he had had his share.

Men and horses sidled out from the butte's cover in the wan light of a half-moon. At first they were careful to make no noise, walking the animals and seeking the soft soils. Then when it seemed the time was right to gently ride the horses, they climbed to saddle leather and headed for a shallow defile where they might be partly hidden. Slowly, barely daring to breathe, wondering how long their luck would last, they made a way across the uneven arid terrain. Some distant hills seemed a good destination but how far could they ride before discovery of their movement came?

The answer arrived pretty soon. Mark Shaw had only relaxed his vigil for some moments and then, staring out into the night again, he spotted the dark shapes of men and riders.

'Kurt! Marshal! They're on the move!'

They sprang from their shallow resting places, three men and a girl, hearts pounding suddenly, grabbing at the horses' reins and hitting the saddles. The animals jigged in swift responses, uncertain at first; then, rowelled with spurs, they leaped into a full lope across the rough land, only the faint light from the moon of any help to them. But it was enough for Kurt's party to spot the escaping desperadoes, who had thrust their own mounts into headlong gallop. The sound of hoof-beats rose into the silent night air with only the inscrutable moon witness to the scene.

Kurt had his Peacemaker in his hard fist, anger boiling in him. These saddle-bums had led them a dance for too long, he figured. Their day of come-uppance was surely overdue.

But as the distance between the rogues and himself lessened, shots rang out, slugs from the killers' handguns, flung into the air with desperate lack of skill. Only terribly bad luck would ensure that a bullet found a target because of the uncertain watery moonlight and the frantic movement of the animals.

Just to give the killers a warning, Kurt snapped off some good shots from his Peacemaker, but luck was with the hardcases and the hot metal was wasted. Mark Shaw threw some good shots, which simply cut the night air; then he concentrated on closing in on the escaping men. Kurt and Mark were way ahead of the marshal and Rose Merit, closing in on Hec Redman and his dirty pals. Kurt aimed carefully, even so his shot was diverted because of the jerking horses. But did find a target, an innocent one.

Hec Redman's horse went down, crashing and

squealing in its fright and then kicking frantically on
its back. The bad man was flung clear and lay dazed.
Kid Curtis suddenly stopped a lucky slug from Mark
Shaw's Colt; he fell and screamed like a child. Rose
chanced a shot at the dark shape of Harry and saw him
plunge from the bucking mount. But the part-Indian
was cunning. He had taken the dive on purpose, figuring a lithe man could snake into some hole and not be
seen, unlike a horse.

When Hec Redman saw Kurt standing over him, he
flung up his gun, still instinctively in his grasp, but
Kurt fired too, a reflex action from his years with guns.
Hec Redman died instantly, a mercy he had never
handed to any of his victims. Kid Curtis writhed in
agony, the slug like a red-hot poker in his flesh. He
rolled to his gun, two yards away on the ground. Jake
Duerr suddenly shot him dead.

'Guess I shouldn't ha' done that!' barked the
marshal.

Harry the 'breed, lay like a rat in a slot in the yellow
earth, silent, dangerous, hoping he could be part of the
desolate land, but luck deserted him when Mark Shaw
came up with Charity and spotted the man. Harry
scuttled but slugs from Mark's gun found their mark,
and wrought a pitiless vengeance.

All at once the night air was silent except for the
blowing horses. Kurt turned away.

'Over, Rose. Billy can rest now. Aw, let's git! I'm sick-
ened!'

When light came they had to bury the cadavers. And
then think about home. Rose was close to Kurt. Charity
and Mark felt even nearer to each other, hands
constantly touching.

Mark tried to laugh. 'Well, I guess we've got the

mystery of the little totem pole to solve. Who knows —
there might be treasure there! What about it, Charity,
my love?'